The Rocker
That
Needs Me

Terri Anne Browning

COPYRIGHT

Other Books By this Author

Reese: A Safe Haven Novella

Reckless With Their Hearts (Duet book with Anna Howard)

The Rocker... Series

The Rocker That Holds Me (Emmie)

The Rocker That Savors Me (Jesse)

Acknowledgement I want to thank my husband for putting up with me while I write this series. He is stuck with all the house cleaning and laundry while I sort through these rocker's lives. Without him I would not have any sanity left to create Demon's Wings for you guys. Special thanks to my BETA readers for giving some insight as the story progressed. I seriously would be lost without them! And lastly to my mom, who finally read one of my books and actually liked it!

Prologue

It was hot as Hell. Muttering a curse under my breath, I tore off my shirt and tossed it on the lawnmower. July was a bitch. Mowing the entire trailer park in the middle of the day wasn't the smartest idea, but it hadn't been my idea. The old cunt that acted as a landlord for the place had wanted it done, and it wasn't my job to question her. She paid me decently for mowing the grass and taking care of the maintenance around the place. I had spent the last three hours mowing and sweating a few gallons along the way. My shirt was soaked, and I seriously needed a shower. After putting the push mower back in the supply shed, I headed home, which was only a few trailers away from the shed sitting in the middle of the rundown trailer park.

Bone tired, I opened the door to my trailer and walked in…

The television was on and Emmie was sitting on my couch. Normally that wouldn't have been a problem for me. When my mom and stepdad weren't home, Emmie came over and watched TV with Shane for a few hours to escape from the nightmare that she called a mother. Today, Shane wasn't home. He was out with some chick that he had met at one of our gigs a few towns over last Friday night.

My mom was at work, like always. She worked hard and was rarely home, so there was only one person that could have let Emmie in…

My heart turned cold, and I had to fight not to throw up as I looked down at the sweet little girl sitting on the sofa. Her hair was a mess, just like it always was. She was wearing shorts that were too big for her, probably a pair that one of us had bought her at a yard sale since her mom didn't care if she had clothes or not. There was a Band-Aid on her shin and a few bruises on her legs and arms.

She looked up at me and smiled when she saw me watching her. "Hey!" she greeted, taking a sip of a juice box.

"Emmie, why are you here?" I asked. "Who let you in?"

Her smile dimmed a little. "Mr. Rusty let me in. I was playing and he asked if I wanted to come in out of the heat."

We were one of the few families in the trailer park that had an air conditioner. *How nice of Rusty to invite Emmie inside to cool off.* I clenched my hands into fists, attempting to stay calm in front of the innocent little girl that I loved so much. I didn't want to scare her, but she had no idea that I had just saved her from unimaginable nightmares.

"Where's Rusty now?"

"He had to use the bathroom," she informed me, watching me closely.

I crouched down in front of her and took her hands in my much larger ones. "Listen to me, Emmie. I want to ask you something, and it's important that you tell me the truth. Okay, sweetheart?"

She nodded her auburn head, and I tightened my hands around hers. "Did..." I swallowed the bile rising in my throat and started again. "Did Rusty touch you?"

Her eyes widened. "I..." She turned pink in the face and bit her lip. "Drake..."

"Did he, Em?" I whispered.

"I...I don't..." She swallowed hard. "He said not to tell."

"Where?" I demanded. "Where did he touch you, Emmie?"

"Just my leg." She had tears in her eyes, and I realized that my hold on her hands was too tight. I eased up on my grip but didn't release her. "He sat with me and rubbed my leg while I watched TV. I didn't like it and told him to stop."

"Did he?"

6

She nodded. "Yes. Of course he did. Then he went to the bathroom. I think he's taking a shower or something cause he's been in there a while."

Rage like nothing I'd ever felt before boiled through me. I was starting to shake with it and saw the fear in Emmie's eyes. I tried to contain it, but I was quickly losing control. "Rusty is a bad man, Emmie. Remember how Jesse, Nik, and I talked to you about bad men?" She nodded her head, tears spilling from her big green eyes. Nine years old and I could already tell that she was going to be one beautiful woman when she grew up.

The guys and I had warned Emmie of a lot of things over the years: not to touch the needles that her mom used for her drug habit and never let one of her mom's men be alone with her. The usual talks that you had with a little kid who lives in a home filled with everyday monsters that kids like Emmie had to deal with.

I had been lucky to never have a parent that abused me or did the things that Emmie's mom did. My mom was great, but she worked two jobs to keep up with bills. My dad was a decent enough guy when he came around, so I hadn't been prepared when my mom had married Rusty Nelson when I was ten and Shane was eight. He had seemed like a good guy too, until the night he had climbed into bed with me. My mom had been working the night shift at the gas station down the road, and Shane had been at a sleepover with his pal from school...

That night had been the beginning of my nightmares. I had been prepared to tell my mom and had threatened to do just that, but Rusty was a manipulative bastard. He could make threats just as good as I could. He had assured me that no one would believe me. Who was going to believe a ten year old boy over an adult like him? Then he had threatened me with the one thing that was sure to keep my mouth shut.

Shane.

7

If I told, then Shane would be next. There was no way I wanted my baby brother, the boy that was my best friend, to experience what I had just gone through. So I kept the abuse to myself. And it continued for nearly a year.

When I turned eleven, I shot up in height by nearly a foot, and puberty hit fast. I didn't look like a little kid anymore. I was turning into a man, and Rusty hadn't liked that, so I was forgotten. I had been scared that the pervert was going to start abusing Shane, so I kept my eyes open for signs that it was going on. There were none and I started to relax...

From down the hall I heard the toilet flush, and I stood, putting the length of the living room between me and Emmie in case I hurt her by accident. There was no way Rusty was walking away from this. He had messed with the wrong kid this time!

"Drake?" Emmie whispered my name, and I gave her a grim smile.

"It's going to be okay, Em." I picked up the phone that was beside the rocker my mom loved to sit in. I punched in a number I knew by heart and waited for someone to pick up on the other end.

"Yeah?" It was Mr. Thornton. The guy sounded drunk and he probably was.

"Mr. Thornton, is Jesse home?" I knew he was. He needed to be at work for the evening shift at the plant soon.

"Jesse!" The old man bellowed, and I heard Jesse stomping through the trailer.

He muttered something I couldn't hear to his dad and then put the phone to his ear. "Dude, I'm busy," Jesse said without even asking who it was. "What do you want?"

I glanced over at Emmie. "I need you to come over. Now."

"Dray, I have to be at work in like twenty minutes."

"Emmie needs you."

8

That stopped him. Of the four of us Jesse was probably the most protective of Emmie. The guy was like a mother bear with her cub. "Is she okay?" he demanded.

"That's questionable." Physically, she was fine. If that douche bag had done nothing more than touch her leg, then she might not have any mental trauma from it. But what I was worried about was her being in the way when I lost control. "Just come over. Run," I told him when I heard the bathroom door open. The phone went dead, and I placed it back in its cradle.

"How about another juice box, Emmie?" Rusty asked as he came down the narrow hallway. "Or a popsicle? That's just what you need on a hot summer day..." He noticed me standing by my mom's chair. "I didn't hear you come in," he muttered.

"I bet." I gave him a once over. He didn't look like a pedophile. He looked like what my mom still thought he was: a decent human being. I guess he was good looking. Rusty had just a hint of a beer gut. His hair was short and free of gray. He was average in height and his southern accent was something that my mom said she liked about him. To me, he was the monster from my nightmares.

The front door opened and Jesse came in looking wild. His gaze went straight to Emmie. "Em? Are you okay?" He rushed over and lifted her into his arms.

"Jesse!" She clung to his neck and buried her face in his chest. "Drake is scaring me."

"What the fuck, man?" Jesse exploded. "She doesn't look any worse than normal..." then he saw my face.

My gaze was still on Rusty, and I knew that my hatred—the pure venomous rage—was burning in my eyes. I was still shaking and it was getting worse by the second. Jesse glanced from me to a very nervous looking Rusty. "Take Emmie outside, Jesse," I told him, not once taking my eyes off my stepfather.

9

"Dray..."

"Now!" I shouted, and Emmie whimpered in his arms. I hated that I was scaring her, but there was nothing I could do about it right now. Later, I promised myself. Later, I would make it up to her.

Jesse murmured something soothingly to Emmie as he turned and left the trailer. With the loud bang from the slamming door, I snapped. There was no way I could hold onto my control now...

I destroyed the living room. The floor lamp that sat beside the old rocker was sticking out of the broken window. The couch I had loved so much was flipped over and would probably never be used again. I thought I heard the dial tone of the phone and figured it was off the hook since the table beside what had once been my mom's favorite chair was in pieces. The place was completely trashed by the time the cops showed up and pulled me off of the unconscious, bleeding man beneath me. It took two of them to put the handcuffs on me while they fought to push my face down into the carpet. One of the cops said something about an ambulance, and I screamed at him to let the fucker die. That only made the cop holding me down dig his knee deeper into my spine.

Shane burst into the trailer, followed by Nik. Neither said a word as they took in the scene. Outside I heard the sirens of the ambulance as I struggled against the cuffs. I wanted to finish what I had started before the paramedics got the chance to save the bastard.

"Drake!" My mom screamed as she followed the EMTs into the trailer. She had just come home from work and stepped into a war zone.

"Drake, what have you done?" She cried when she saw her husband lying motionless on her living room floor and me, her oldest son, in handcuffs. "Why did you do this?"

I clenched my jaw and refused to meet her eyes. "Because that piece of shit deserved it."

10

"Mom!" Shane grabbed our mother. "Mom, there's something you need to know."

Something in my little brother's voice made me glance over at him. He held onto Mom's hands and spoke softly to her, but I still heard. "Rusty molested me when I was nine," he explained, and I lost it.

All of it for nothing! The years of keeping the secret that haunted me night and day to protect him. I had turned to drinking myself to death just to sleep at night. And it was all for nothing! Rusty had still done to Shane what he had done to me.

I bucked the cops off me and somehow got to my feet despite the cuffs. Before I could reach Rusty, a third cop tackled me.

"No!" I screamed. "I'm going to kill him!"

Rusty Nelson was going to die for touching my little brother...

Chapter 1

Drake

I woke with the taste of stale Jack Daniels on my tongue, my head pounding and fighting the urge to vomit.

Yeah, my typical morning!

Nothing special about that or the nightmares that still lingered in my mind. They were what made me run for the bathroom. I barely made it before I started retching and emptied my dinner from the night before into the toilet.

I was brushing my teeth when Emmie waddled into my connecting bathroom and glared at me. Apparently she was still mad at me, and I still had no clue why. Damn pregnancy hormones!

"Grab a shower. You're helping Jesse move Layla and her sisters into the guest house today."

I groaned. "Emmie, my head is about to split open."

"How is that different from any other day?" she called over her shoulder as she left the bathroom. "Hurry up. Jesse is leaving soon."

Muttering a curse, I stepped into the shower. Thirty minutes later, I was riding shotgun in a rental with Jesse. He knew my head was killing me, and he didn't talk much because of it. I rested my head against the back of the seat and prayed that the day would pass quickly. All I wanted was some Jack and a bed.

The apartment duplex Jesse pulled up in front of wasn't the most seedy place I had ever seen, but it wasn't the nicest either. We weren't exactly in gang territory, but it was obvious that this wasn't the safest of neighborhoods. I was kind of glad that Layla was moving into the guest house after seeing this place. I liked her and wanted her somewhere safer.

The sun was bright and I regretted not wearing my sunglasses as I climbed the stairs to the second floor behind Jesse. He knocked and the door opened.

"Jesse, hey," Layla's raspy voice greeted the drummer.

I stood there in the glaring sun and watched them devour each other with their eyes. Yeah, there wasn't anything going on there! "Sometime today, Jesse. Stop eye fucking the chick and let's get this show started, man." Layla's cheeks flushed, and she stepped back to let us into the apartment. "I wasn't expecting you guys to help me."

I dropped down on a couch that reminded me of the one my mom had loved so much when I was a kid. This one was probably as old as I was.

"Neither were we," I muttered.

"What Drake means is that he is here under duress. This is his punishment for pissing Emmie off last night," Jesse informed her.

"I still don't understand what I did," I grumbled. "One minute she's all smiles and the next she's screaming at me." I shook my head and my long hair fell in my face. "I hate pregnancy hormones. Cannot wait for that demon child to get out of her!" I wanted my sweet little Emmie back.

Okay, she wasn't sweet, but she was ours, and I wouldn't trade her for anyone else. But lately she wasn't the same girl that the guys and I had practically raised. She had been taken over by the spawn growing in her belly.

Layla laughed and it was a sweet sound. "That isn't going to help," she assured me. "After the baby is born, she's going to be worse. Take my word for it, sweetie. Postpartum is worse than the mood swings she's having now."

"Ah, hell," Jesse muttered at the same time I did.

"Hey, Layla, did you already pack the bathroom? I need…" My head snapped around at the sound of that voice, and I was sure that my heart stopped in my chest when I met the whiskey colored eyes of an angel. Her long, midnight black hair was pulled back in a ponytail. Her brown-amber eyes were huge in her beautiful face. She had plump lips that were almost bee stung and a nose that was tipped at the end. The angel was tall, her waist long and slender, but she had curves that made my body ache to hold her against me.

This angel was young; I would say no more than twenty-one...Layla introduced the angel. "Lana, this is Jesse and that's Drake. Guys, this is my *seventeen* year old sister, Lana."

Seventeen. Seventeen. SEVENTEEN!

Seven-fucking-teen!

The number bounced around in my already throbbing head, and I thought I was going to go mad from it. No! Not seventeen. She had to be older. I couldn't be attracted in a seventeen year old girl.

"It's nice to meet you, Lana," Jesse said as he stared at the angel.

I was fascinated by the pretty pink that flooded her cheeks. "Yeah, you too," she murmured and glanced at her sister. "Layla, can you help me with something in the bathroom?"

The sisters left us alone in the living room, and Jesse dropped down on the sofa beside of me. "Dude, you look pale."

I wasn't surprised. I think I had actually felt the color drain from my face when Layla had said the word *seventeen*. I felt sick to my stomach for an entirely different reason than the ones that I had woken up to.

"Are you really demons?"

I turned my head to find a little girl with long, curly, dark hair standing a few feet from the sofa. She had big dark eyes and a cute little button nose, and just like Emmie had all those years ago, this little girl sucked me in. I couldn't help smiling at her. "No, sweetheart. I'm not really a demon." All though some people had likened me to one a few times. The public eye thought I was some hard-ass with no heart or soul.

Mostly, they were right. Unless you counted Emmie and my band brothers, I had no love and no compassion for anyone.

"What's your name?" The little girl asked.

"I'm Drake," I told her. "He's Jesse."

Her dark eyes took us both in as if she were assessing us both. Then, with a trust that only the young and innocent had, she climbed onto my lap. "I'm Lucy. It's nice to meet you, Mr. Drake."

"It's a pleasure to meet you too, Lucy."

For the next five minutes, she asked a hundred questions about the house she was going to be living in. Before Jesse or I could attempt to answer, she threw another one at us. Within the first minute, I knew that her favorite word was *awesome*. She wanted to build a sandcastle but had never been to the beach. Before I could really think about it, I offered to teach her.

Layla came out of the bedroom with a smile on her face. "Not today, Lucy," she told the girl. "We have a lot to do today, baby."

"Tomorrow?" she asked.

I was already nodding my head. It sounded like fun the more I thought about it. Fuck, I don't think I had ever made a sandcastle either, but I wanted to make one with Lucy. "Tomorrow. It's a date, okay?"

Her eyes grew wide. "Promise?"

I smiled. "Promise. Now, let's get you ladies moved."

Lana

I knew who Demon's Wings were. Layla was a big fan of their music, but I would have known about them even if she wasn't. They were an incredible rock band, and even I liked some of their songs, which was saying a lot because my tastes leaned toward musicians like Michael Bublé.

Lately, the band had been in the tabloids, which wasn't typical of them. They mostly kept a low profile, but the front man, Nikolas Armstrong, was going to be a father, and that was a big deal in the music world. He had knocked up the band's surrogate sister and caused heads to turn all around the world. The tabloids had made a killing off the story for months now, but it had died down for the most part. I figured that when that baby was born the band would be hounded yet again.

The baby story was the first real news about the band in a few years or so. The last time they had made tabloid news it was because of Drake Stevenson. The man was reported to be some psycho who had thrown a doctor through a window. The picture of the bad-ass rocker glaring at the photographer, who had dared to take his picture, had shown a man that looked beyond wild and dangerous. I guess you could understand my shock at finding that same guy standing in what had been my living room for the past two years. I was nervous at first, especially when he looked at me and I felt as if he was looking straight to my soul. But even though he scared the crap out of me, I was sure that my heart was racing for reasons other than fear.

Damn, that man was sexy! You could even go as far as saying that he was beautiful. His face was all hard lines and angles, but each angle looked as if the Gods themselves had sculpted each line. Adonis, the God of beauty and desire, had nothing on Drake Stevenson, and with just one look, my breath felt like it was trapped in my lungs.

What shocked me more was that over the next few hours I found myself no longer afraid of him. He went out of his way to make Lucy laugh. Every time I picked up something heavy, he quickly took it away from me and carried it to the truck himself. Drake the rock star might be a total prick, but apparently Drake the man was a gentleman.

I felt as if there was an invisible force pushing me toward him. Normally, I would have put on the E-brake fast. Rock stars were bad news. I had grown up with one after another

16

warming my mother's bed. I had seen firsthand how they treated people, and it wasn't pretty. But for some reason I felt like Drake and Jesse were different.

Just as I felt that Shane and Nik were different when I met them later that day as they helped us unload the moving truck. They were all really nice, and I felt comfortable around them all. And Emmie? She reminded me of Layla a little. Someone who didn't let anyone walk all over her, who didn't let the world pull her down.

By the end of the day, I found myself crushing on Drake. It was crazy. He was thirty one, and I was seventeen. Sure, rockers dated younger women all the time, but I wasn't going to be some rocker's Priscilla to his Elvis. Nope, not going to happen!

Sunday was my homework day. I normally didn't mind doing homework. Layla was a hard-ass about getting good grades, and it came easy for me. I studied hard and took extra classes. Since I had been living with Layla and I no longer had to spend so much time taking care of Lucy—something I had done from the day she was born up until our loser mother had died—I started taking the extra credit classes my high school offered. The classes were basic general studies classes for college, and at the end of this term I would have enough college credits to qualify as a sophomore when I actually started college.

Monday, I drove to school by myself for the first time. Layla was awesome. She was letting me drive her old Corolla so I didn't have to transfer schools. It wasn't that I would miss my friends; I spent so much time at school either studying or participating in the mandatory sports program—I had chosen track because I sucked at team sports—I didn't have any friends. Not one.

Of course not having friends made it hard at school sometimes. None of the girls liked me because they either: *A*-thought I was a stuck up bitch because I refused to let them suck me into the everyday drama that tended to be a teenage girls life; or *B*- they thought I wanted their man. My answer was always *C*. I didn't have time for anyone's drama but my own, and I wouldn't touch their boyfriends if they paid me. Not having friends had given me time to observe the goings-on of others around me, and I had discovered that most of the *boyfriends* that I was accused of *wanting* were total tools and were getting more side action than their girlfriends realized.

The day before, Layla had bought two new phones. She had given Lucy her old one in case of emergencies, but I got my own, along with an unlimited text plan to go with the internet and call plan. Of course I had given my number to Drake. I wasn't sure how it had happened, but we had ended up texting back and forward until after midnight last night. And today, even though I knew he was supposed to be in the studio working on new material with the other guys of Demon's Wings, we had been texting regularly.

During English he sent me a funny picture of his brother goofing off at lunch. Because I hadn't been expecting it, I didn't think to control my snort of laughter while my teacher was giving a boring lecture on the importance of a strong introduction to an essay. I hadn't been paying attention because I had already taken college English 101 and passed it with an A. The only reason I was even in the guy's class was because I had to have it to graduate.

"Miss Daniels, is there something you would like to share with the class?" The jerk asked in a nasally voice that always grates down my spine. Mr. Mills was in his late twenties with a Justin Bieber haircut, and most of the girls in the school squealed like the little girls they were when they found out they would have him for English. I wasn't one of his fans and hadn't made a secret of it—ever. Of course I felt like he didn't like me and was always trying to single me out in embarrassing ways.

I slipped my phone between my book and notebook to hide it from the teacher. "No, Mr. Mills," I assured him.

"Then perhaps you would like to tell us the best way to start a Compare/Contrast introduction." His smirk told me he thought I couldn't give him a good enough answer to satisfy him.

He was a little more pissy toward me than usual by the end of the class, after my five minute explanation for his question. When the bell rang, I was more than happy to grab my things and get out of the way. I ducked into the girls' room before heading to my last class of the day and texted Drake back.

You made me LOL in English! Prick teacher hates me.

Within seconds Drake texted me back. *Fuck! Sorry, Angel!*

Don't worry about it. See you later. □

That evening when I got home, Layla was more quiet than usual. Last night she had asked me about Drake, and I had shrugged it all off. He was my friend—my only friend! I wasn't about to let her step in and ruin it because she felt like I couldn't handle myself; even if my feelings for the rocker were stronger than mere friendship. I brushed it off as just a silly infatuation.

After dinner, I texted Drake to ask if he wanted to come enjoy the night air with me. It was still warm out at night, and I was feeling suffocated inside the guest house. When he texted me back saying that he would be right out, I gathered up a sheet and all the little candles we had.

By the time he met me in the yard, which separated the guesthouse from the main house, I had it all set up. It looked romantic and I had to keep reminding myself that nothing about Drake and my relationship was romantic. He would run for the hills if he knew I was crushing on him, and really I couldn't blame him. He must have had plenty of that drama in his life being a rocker.

Drake surprised me when he produced a sketch book and a set of charcoal sketching pencils. "Can I draw you?" he asked, sounding a little unsure.

"Sure. If you want to...I didn't know you could draw." I arranged myself on the sheet so I could watch him over the sketch pad while he worked.

His fingers moved fast and with obvious skill. I ached to see what he was drawing. The concentration on his face as he watched me made me ache for a different reason altogether.

"It's something I do as a stress reliever," he said after a few minutes. "Art was my favorite class in school. For my eighth birthday my dad got me a professional art kit. It had paint and charcoal and a million other things that an eight year old doesn't understand how to use." He smiled and I could see the little boy that he had been shining in those blue-gray eyes. "My mom argued that it was too expensive, that it would be destroyed by the end of the day, but I took care of it and found that I really liked using the charcoal to draw. When I was thirteen, I entered an art festival in town and actually won a hundred dollars by coming in second place in the art show."

"Wow. I can maybe draw a convincing stick figure if I had to," He laughed. It was a gut-deep laugh that made me so happy it had come from something I said. He didn't seem like the type of guy that laughed often.

"So if art isn't your talent what is?" he asked as he continued to draw.

My attention kept going to his hands—those long, slender fingers as they moved with sure strokes across the sketch pad. "I like to dance," I told him. "And I'm a decent long distance runner."

He cocked a brow at my answer. "Dance?"

I nodded. "Yeah, I love to dance. When I was little, before my mom kicked Layla out, Layla would take me to this little dance academy when she got home from school. I got to learn tap dancing, ballet, and jazz. I'm a big jazz and swing fan."

20

Drake grinned. "So you like Michael Bublé and Sarah Brickel. Maybe Robbie Williams?" I shrugged and he leaned forward, tapping me on the end of the nose with a finger. "There's nothing wrong with liking them. I've met Michael Bublé a few times at the Grammys. Nice enough guy."

"I might have every song of his on my iPod." I shrugged again. "Who is your rock hero?" I asked, determined to know every little thing about this man. Just being with him like this, talking about nothing more important than our tastes in music, was perfect. I wanted to freeze time and hold onto this moment for the rest of my life.

"Keith Richards was always my hero." He was back to concentrating on his sketchpad. "The man has talent. When I was twelve I mowed grass for an entire summer and saved up to buy my first guitar. I taught myself how to play it by watching and listening to Keith Richards. That's how we got started. I was Keith and Nik was Mick Jagger. We were just playing around. But then Jesse and Shane joined us, and we actually sounded pretty good. We started playing at parties for the kids at school. From there it was bars close to home. When I was twenty-one some talent scout heard us and told Rich, our manager, about us. A week later, we were on a tour bus, officially rock stars."

"That's wild!" I pulled my knees up against my chest and rested my chin on them. My hair fell in my face, and I pushed it back. "Is it all you hoped for? All you ever wanted?" Pain crossed his face. Drake grew quiet and I wondered if he was going to answer me when he finally shook his head. "No. It isn't all I ever wanted. After the first year or so, I was already burned out. I want more from life than rock-and-roll. We all do now. Don't get me wrong, Lana, I love making music. I love the thrill of playing for a crowd. But I hate the life that comes with it."

Chapter 2

Drake

I wasn't sure why I was so drawn to Lana. I tried to stay away. For about a minute, I succeeded, but I found that it physically hurt to stay away. I refused to give my feelings any name other than friendship. Being friends was safe. I could work with that. So what if just looking at her made me ache deep inside in a way I couldn't ever remember aching before.

She drew me in and I went willingly. Lana, my sweet, beautiful angel, was easy to talk to. I found myself confiding in her about things no one else knew. I hadn't even admitted hating the fast pace of the rock-and-roll world that I had gotten caught up in all those years ago to Emmie. With Lana it just came naturally.

I spent every evening with her. Talking about the stupidest things, getting to know a girl—fuck anyone—just for the hell of it. Some nights we would just sit and I would sketch the angel. Others we would lie on the beach and listen as the waves crashed against the beach. With each wave that hit the beach, I felt as if I was being washed in the sweetest peace. It was soothing to be with her. I was able to go without a whole bottle of Jack Daniels to help me fall asleep for an entire week. When I woke each morning I wasn't drenched in sweat like I normally was. Of course I still had the nightmares. I doubted I would ever be free of them, but that week they didn't haunt me like they normally did.

Friday, I took Lana to dinner. There was a great little Greek restaurant that I loved. I picked her up, refusing to think of it as a date. I had never taken a girl on a date in my life, and I wasn't about to think of this time out with Lana as one. That just screamed *wrong* to me.

It was fun. I enjoyed every second of it and dreaded the time that I would have to take her home. After dinner I found a park, and we sat on the swings just talking like we always did. I had only known this girl a week, and yet she probably knew as much about me as Emmie did. Well, except for the parts that I refused to tell Lana. I didn't want to put those images in her innocent mind.

And maybe I was scared that if my angel knew about my past she would be too disgusted to want to continue with our friendship.

I drove us back to Malibu in the Escalade. When I pulled into the driveway it was just after ten. Instead of getting out right away, Lana turned toward me and smiled that smile of hers, which I still hadn't been able to get perfect on paper. There was something about that smile, the way it filled me with so much peace. There was a hint of mischief that sparkled in those whiskey eyes of hers that calmed my need for the bottle, at least for the most part.

"Thanks for tonight, Drake," she said. "It was fun."

"Would you like to go shopping with me tomorrow?" I didn't know where the idea had come from. What the fuck did I know about shopping? I had a shit load of money and had barely touched a cent of it. Emmie took care of my bills and bought everything I needed. I guess I was a little helpless when it came to certain things, but I wanted to spoil Lana. Friends could do that, right?

"Shopping?" She raised a brow and grinned. "You want to take me shopping?"

I shrugged. "Yeah. Bring Lucy. We can make a day of it." I wanted to spend every minute possible with her. Maybe she was a new addiction—one that brought me more peace than the bottle did.

Somehow we ended up talking for nearly an hour, just sitting in the SUV, talking about something I doubted I would remember in the morning. I made her laugh and it was like bells ringing in my ears—the best music I had ever heard.

When I next looked at the clock on the dashboard it was a little after eleven. She was just as reluctant, if not more so, to end the night. I reached out and pushed her long, midnight black hair away from her beautiful face. My fingers burned where they touched her flawless skin. After only a small hesitation, I leaned in and brushed a soft kiss over her cheek. "Good night, Lana," I murmured.

Pink filled her cheeks and she bit her lip. "G-goodnight Drake," she whispered and slipped out of the Escalade. I waited until she was out of sight before getting out. I needed the time to calm my racing heart and aching body.

When I entered the house, Shane had gone out—not that it was a big surprise. I shuddered a little at the possible places my little brother could have been tonight. The bottle might have been my crutch, but Shane's addiction was worse in my book. His constant need to have sex—the orgies, the sex clubs—was going to kill him long before the bottle pickled my liver. Emmie insisted that we all get tested regularly, mostly because of Shane.

Jesse and Nik were sprawled out on the sectional with beers in their hands, and Emmie snuggled up to Nik. It had taken me a little while to get used to the sight of Emmie with Nik. It wasn't that I didn't like the idea of them together. It was just hard to see her as anything other than our sweet little Emmie. Now, I was forced to see her for what she was. A sexy woman who was serious with one of my scumbag band brothers.

Her belly was peeking out of her Demon's Wings shirt, and I cringed at the thought of the little spawn growing inside of her. That little demon child made my Emmie evil at times. When she saw me, her big green eyes lit up and Nik helped her stand. She wrapped her arms around me and wanted to know all about my night out, but I wasn't ready to tell her about it. For now, I wanted to keep the time I had spent with Lana locked inside, holding onto it for as long as I could before

I shared it with Emmie. I hated to admit it but I was probably the least closest with Emmie and it was my fault.

I loved her and would lay down my life for her, but because of what had happened all those years ago, I held a part of myself back, even from her...

Shopping with Lana and Lucy was fun. I was enjoying watching Lana try on clothes that looked as if they were made just for her.

The fun ended when I bought all the clothes that Lana tried on and a couple pair of shoes. She exploded on me and became the fierce little bitch that lurked under the surface of all her angelic beauty. I refused to let my body respond to the sight of how incredibly sexy she looked spitting mad. Instead, I got mad too.

Lana stormed out of the exclusive boutique while I finished paying for the clothes and accessories. Lucy sighed and shook her head but helped me carry the bags to the Escalade. We gave each other the silent treatment while shopping for Lucy.

When I pulled into the driveway a few hours later, Lana jumped out without so much as a word. I followed behind her, and Lucy, weighed down with all the bags from the shopping expedition, walked at a slower pace. Layla met us at the door. Lucy was already talking a mile a minute about the day.

The bedroom door slammed shut just as I entered the guest house, and I glared at the closed door. Even though I was steaming mad, I still wanted to be close to her. And now that stubborn little brat—really she was a bitch sometimes!—hadn't even let me tell her goodnight.

"Lucy, go watch some cartoons," Layla told the still bubbling Lucy. "You can tell me all about your day later. I promise."

"Okay." Lucy sighed. "Don't yell at Drake. It isn't his fault that Lana is so rotten."

I dropped the bags on the floor. "How was your day?" Layla asked, and I heard the amusement in her voice.

I turned my glare from the closed door to Layla. There was a ghost of a smile on her face. "Your sister is so stubborn," I told her.

Her lips twitched into a full blown grin. "I'm sure it wasn't that bad."

"She didn't want me to buy her anything. Nothing! Not one little thing. Then, when I bought them anyway, she stormed out of the store and left me there with poor little Lucy. She refused to speak to me the rest of the afternoon..." I broke off, running a hand through my hair and pulling on the ends. I probably looked demented or something, but that was the way I felt right then. "She makes me f..." I stopped before the curse word left my lips and corrected myself. "Freaking bonkers!"

"Give her a little while. She won't stay mad forever." Layla assured me with an encouraging smile. "Lana's the type of girl that doesn't want material things. She learned the hard way that people trying to buy her affections doesn't exactly mean that they care about her."

My heart clenched at her words. Lana had told me a little about her childhood, but like me, she had mostly evaded the subject. The last thing I wanted to do was treat her like some douche bag from her past.

"She would rather you stop and pick her a flower beside the road than buy her one from the flower shop."

"I wasn't...I just wanted..." I raked a hand through my hair again, stopping the flow of words that didn't make sense. I guess I had really fucked up, and I felt a little nauseated that I had hurt Lana, even if it was unintentional. "I'll call her later," I muttered.

I couldn't sleep that night. All I wanted to do was text Lana, but I knew she needed a little while to calm down. To keep myself from picking up my phone, I swallowed a fifth of Jack and let the numbness take me off to nightmare land for the night. I woke at dawn in a pool of sweat and rising bile in the back of my throat.

When I had my shit together, I forced down some breakfast and finally pulled out my phone. My fingers didn't hesitate as they raced over the keys.

I'm sorry.

I didn't do that often. There wasn't much I felt I should apologize for, but I knew I had been wrong this time. I should have listened to her when she said she didn't want me to buy her anything.

A full minute went by before my phone buzzed. I glanced down to see the message across the screen and felt the tightness around my heart ease.

I'm sorry, too! I was a bitch.

My hands hovered over the keys. ***Can I come over?***

I was hoping you would.

I tossed my cereal bowl in the sink. It took me exactly two minutes to get through the house, cross the patio and small yard, and knock on the front door of the guesthouse. My knuckles barely touched the door before it opened and Lana was throwing herself into my arms. "I'm sorry," she whispered.

Wrapping my arms around her small waist, I held her tight for a moment and breathed in the sweet scent of her shampoo and the lotion she always seemed to be putting on. Lana didn't do perfume. Her fingers combed through my hair, and I closed my eyes tight, basking in the peaceful feeling of having her in my arms for the first time.

"I hate fighting with you," I muttered as I set her on her feet. "I'm not sure I'd survive if I really pissed you off."

A small smile tugged at the corners of her bee-stung lips. "Nah. You can handle it."

I grinned. "Let's not find out, okay?"

"I'll do my best." She rolled her whiskey colored eyes at me, and I smacked her on the ass as she turned into the living room. Her squeal was music to my ears. I picked her up and tossed her on the couch and then spent the next five minutes tickling her until she had tears running down her cheeks. I didn't normally get so close to her, but my relief at making up with her after our fight was too overwhelming for me not to find a reason to touch her.

Our playing woke Lucy up, and I spent the rest of the day just hanging out with them. Around noon Lana started getting worried about Layla, and we went over to the main house to ask Emmie if she had heard from either Layla or Jesse. I figured that Jesse had been unable to contain his feelings the night before and the two were shacked up in a hotel room somewhere, but I didn't dare speak my thoughts aloud.

After Emmie assured her that she would call Jesse and make sure they were okay, I talked Lana into a swim. It wasn't hard to do, but after seeing her in her bikini for the first time, I was seriously regretting my decision to spend a few hours by the pool. What sick bastard invented bikinis anyway? Lucky for me Lucy made a great chaperone, and I was able to keep my reactions in check for the most part.

When I found myself drooling at the sight of Lana's chest in the lemon yellow top barely containing her curves, I knew it was time to order some dinner. Anything to get some clothes on my angel so I wasn't constantly in a state of pain from just looking at her.

A movie and some good Chinese rounded out the day. I didn't want to go back to the main house, but I knew that staying wasn't an option. Lana and Lucy both had school the next morning, and I had to go into the studio. I placed a kiss on top of Lucy's dark, curly head and one on Lana's cheek. "I'll text you," I promised.

"Okay." She bit her lip and I saw the disappointment in her eyes. She was just as reluctant for me to leave as I was to be going. "Thanks for dinner."

By the time I reached the house, my chest felt like I had an elephant sitting on it. I raced up to my room and found one of my fifths and swallowed a third of it in one go. I was used to the burn as it flooded my throat. The heat as it hit my stomach was a welcoming distraction from the pressure around my heart, and I dropped down on the edge of my bed before swallowing another third.

I didn't want to be alone, so I ended up on the sectional, watching football with Nik and Shane. They didn't say anything as I sat down between them and swallowed some more of my Jack. The bottle was nearly gone, and I was still feeling like I couldn't breathe. Fuck! I hated this feeling. All because I couldn't stand to be away from a girl I had no business having anything but brotherly feelings for!

Jesse came home sometime later. I wasn't exactly sure what time it was. By then, I had found a second bottle of Jack Daniels and started chasing it with beer. I had no idea what was going on with the football game and no clue as to who was even playing. I was numb but still unable to breathe.

When the bottle was empty, Jesse helped me up to my room and I fell onto my bed. "So what happened?" he asked as he pulled off my shoes. "You and Lana have a fight?"

"Yesterday..." I told him about the shopping trip and the argument we had had. "But I 'pologized to...day."

"She didn't forgive you?"

"Nah. She did. Spent rest...the day 'er...and Wucy." My words were getting slurred and I tried to concentrate on forming them. Not that it mattered, all my band brothers had spent so much time around me in a drunken state that they had picked up the language. "One of... best days of my wife," I admitted.

"So why the fuck are you drinking?" Jesse demanded.

I glared at him. Was he crazy? How could he not know why I was drinking? Was he blind? "'Cause I want 'er so fuckin' much! 'Cause I feel like I need 'er to breathe. 'Cause she is seventeen fuckin' years old!" I shouted.

The drummer dropped down on the edge of my bed. "Dray, she's beautiful. A blind man could see how beautiful she is. And it isn't just on the outside. She's really sweet, man. Lana is special."

I knew all of that. It made all my feelings that much more intense. Lana was my angel. And I couldn't touch her. "I know that," I whispered.

"And I think she has some strong feelings for you too."

I knew that too, but for Lana it was just a crush. A girl her age couldn't understand the feelings I had. I couldn't imagine her feeling for me what I felt for her. No, I refused to even think about it. I was her friend. That was all.

"What are you going to do?" Jesse asked after a few minutes.

I scrubbed a hand over my wet eyes. "Nothin'."

"Nothing? So you just go on being friends, but killing yourself with alcohol to numb your pain?"

I shrugged or at least thought I did. "I can't touch 'er. I *won't* touch 'er!"

"Have you at least talked to her about this?" Jesse demanded, sounding frustrated.

"No. She's too young ter understand. I'm not going ter burden 'er with it." I didn't want to put my nightmares in her head. That ugliness didn't belong inside my angel's mind. "Shanks for taking care of me, man..." I attempted to say as I let myself float off to sleep...

The dreams haunted my sleep. The fight, the gun shots... Emmie crawled into bed with me, holding me close and whispering things that I couldn't make sense of through the drunken haze. My tears dried and the shaking in my limbs slowly faded. Her presence alone soothed some of my pain, her fingers stroking through my hair like a lifeline connecting me to the present.

As I drifted back off to sleep, the dream was still waiting to consume me, but it took a different turn than usual. Instead of a nine year old Emmie sitting on my couch, it was Lana. She smiled up at me in that mysterious angelic way of hers, but it didn't calm me like it normally did.

The trailer was dark, the heat from the summer pressing in on us as Rusty came down the hall. He said something and I watched as Lana turned to me with a disgusted look on her face. Then she faded from the couch as if she had never been there...

Chapter 3

Lana

I should have known it was going to be a sucky day the second I woke up.

The sound of the alarm only made me groan. Since we had moved to Malibu I had to get up an hour earlier so I could get to school on time. Normally I would shower, but this morning I wasn't in the mood to get my hair wet. I climbed out of bed and went into the bathroom. As I passed the sink, the mirror caught my attention and I saw the effects of a sleepless night.

After falling into bed last night, I hadn't been able to get to sleep. Instead, I had stared at my cellphone, mentally willing Drake to text me. I didn't know why, but I had this ache in my gut and a weight around my heart. Once or twice I was sure that I was actually having a panic attack. I had never experienced something like that.

Something deep inside told me that Drake needed me, and I wasn't sure how I could help. If I went over to the main house and told them that I couldn't sleep because I was scared something was wrong with Drake they'd think I was a freak. Having gotten to know Shane a little over the last week, I knew that he would only laugh at me.

But the feeling hadn't gone away, and I tossed and turned all night, finally falling into a restless sleep only an hour or so before the alarm went off.

I brushed my teeth and washed my face. Not in the mood to put on makeup. I didn't like to wear it anyway, I pulled my hair back into a pony tail and added a headband to keep the stray strands out of my face. Picking up my backpack from the bedroom floor, I found Layla's car keys and headed for the door.

Layla came out of the kitchen, a package of Pop-tarts and a small bottle of orange juice in her hands. "Drive carefully," she told me with a warm smile.

For some reason tears burned my eyes, and I could only nod as I left the guesthouse. Layla was my rock. She had been the mother I needed when I was growing up. The day that our mom tossed her out was the worst day of my life. I cried myself to sleep for six months, wanting my sister to tuck me in because Mom wouldn't. I was only nine, but within a week I was doing things that some grown women didn't even know how to do—like cooking my own dinner and washing my own clothes.

Just before Mom died she and I had been arguing a lot. I was scared to death that she was ready to kick me out too. Lucy was still so young, so defenseless. It sounds inhumane but I had breathed a sigh of relief when Lydia Daniels died. Moving in with Layla had been the best thing to happen to me since the day I had last seen her.

I was five minutes late for my first class because traffic was so horrible that morning. The teacher let me off with a warning and a lecture on punctuality. Really, I would have rather taken the detention than hear that bag of hot air preaching to me. At lunch I had to settle on a bag of chips and a bottle of water because nothing the lunch ladies had fixed looked edible. Of course Mr. Mills was his usual douche bag self to me during English. I was about five seconds away from telling that prick off when my phone vibrated.

Glancing down at my desk, I saw a text from Drake.

Wanna grab dinner later? Me, you and Shane?

Definitely! I quickly answered back.

I thought my shitty day was over until I got into Layla's car after school and the damned thing refused to start. Muttering a few choice curses that would land me a scolding from my sister, I popped the hood on the old car then wondered what I had expected to accomplish by doing that. I wasn't exactly mechanically inclined!

I thought about calling Layla but knew that she wouldn't know what to do any more than I did. Fishing out my phone from my back pocket, I texted Drake.

Know anything about cars?

A little.

Layla's car won't start... I texted, not sure if I was asking him to be my white knight or not...

On my way, Angel!

My heart turned all mushy when he had quickly come to my rescue without me really even asking. It took him thirty minutes to get to my school. A taxi pulled up beside me and both Drake and Shane stepped out. I was one of three cars left in the parking lot. As soon as I saw them, I got out of the car. I put the time to good use by finishing up my Calculus homework while I waited.

Shane had a backwards ball cap on his shaggy head and sunglasses over his eyes. Drake was sporting some scruff on his sexy jaw, and I was almost hypnotized by him. "Thanks for coming. Sorry to pull you guys away from the studio."

"You're more important," Drake said, making my heart melt all over again. "Are you okay?"

"I'm fine. Layla's car on the other hand? Well, I'll leave it to you guys to determine that."

Shane fiddled with some wires, checked some fluid levels, and then tried to start the engine. It did more for him than it had for me by making a gravely noise, but it still didn't start. He pushed his glasses up on top of his hat and shook his head. His dangerous good looks were startling when you had those blue-gray eyes looking right at you. He and Drake looked so much alike they could have passed for twins at first glance. Drake was a few inches taller than his brother, but Shane was wider in the shoulders.

"I'll get it towed," Shane said after he told me what he thought was wrong with it. I didn't really understand anything that had come out of his mouth, but I knew that it wasn't a good thing.

"Great," I muttered. "How am I going to get to school tomorrow?"

"We can drop you off before we go into the studio," Drake assured me. I started to argue that it would be too far out of their way, but he gave me a look that told me I was best to keep my mouth shut. Not wanting to start another fight when the last one had left me miserable, I just nodded.

The tow truck arrived, and Shane called a taxi for us. I had already texted Layla with what was going on so she wouldn't worry that I was so late getting home. But apparently she had already known about the car trouble and that the Stevenson brothers were helping me out.

"Let's grab something to eat before we go home," Shane suggested. "I'm freaking starving."

"I could eat," Drake agreed. "What do you feel like eating, Angel?"

I sat between them in the back of the taxi, leaning into Drake more so I could have an excuse to touch him. "I don't care. Anything sounds good right now." It was almost dinner time, and I was running on a Pop-tart and a bag of chips. I was hungry enough to be borderline ravenous.

The little Italian place that Shane picked was amazing. I ate all of my Chicken Parmesan and was still hungry, so I started picking off of Drake's plate. His Triple Trio of lasagna, bruschetta, and shrimp with spaghetti was amazing. The company was even better than the food. Just being with Drake eased something deep inside of me. I enjoyed being around Shane almost as much. He had a way of making me laugh when I didn't want to.

As we lingered over dessert—some kind of incredible Tiramisu that made me moan on the first bite—I found that I didn't want the evening to end. The day in general had sucked, but the evening couldn't have been more perfect if I had tried. I tried to make every bite of dessert last a little longer.

"Don't you like it?" Shane asked as he took his last bite.

"It's delicious," I assured him.

"Got a text from Jesse," Drake said as he dropped down in his chair after having come back from the bathroom. "We aren't going into the studio tomorrow or the rest of the week. Emmie had to go to the doctor this morning and she has to rest." His brow was wrinkled in concern. "The doctor is still talking about a C-section."

"Well she is kind of tiny, Dray." Shane tossed back the rest of his wine. "And if that kid is anything like Nik, she's going to have a huge head. This will probably be better for Em."

"I guess," Drake muttered, swallowing the last of his coffee. "I guess I'm just terrified of the unknown."

"She's in the best hands, bro. You know Nik wouldn't let her be in anything but." His words were to offer comfort, but I wondered if he was trying to comfort himself too.

I knew that Emmie was special to the four members of Demon's Wings. She was the sun that they all seemed to revolve around. I loved that they could feel so deeply for her. It showed me that beneath the badass rocker persona they were good guys. Up until I met them I had thought that all rockers were the same. Douche bags and assholes. Mom's life had shown me that side of the rocker world, and I had hated every second of it. Drake and his band brothers had proved to me that there were some good guys floating around in the rock world after all.

"Do you have homework?" Drake surprised me by changing the subject.

I shook my head. "I finished my Calculus while I waited for you two to show up."

36

"Think Layla would get mad if we didn't go straight home?" He was pulling his wallet out and tossing a few large bills on the table.

Had he read my mind? I wasn't ready to go home either. "She texted me and told me that she was having dinner with Jesse. They're taking Lucy out for mac and cheese."

Shane laughed. "He loves his mac and cheese. Now he has an excuse to get it as often as possible."

"Let's go to a movie," Drake suggested. "I haven't been to a movie in forever."

Shane snorted. "No thanks." He stood. "Since we aren't going into the studio tomorrow. I'm going to find something a little more X-rated to keep me occupied." Drake muttered something under his breath, causing Shane to laugh. "You got it, bro."

"Don't make Emmie worry. Come home tonight."

"I'll do my best." But Shane was still grinning. He placed a kiss on top of my head. "Have fun. See you later."

"Bye, Shane." I watched him go and then turned back to the big man seated across from me. "Still want to see a movie?"

"If you feel up to it." But I could tell he was really looking forward to going to see one. The idea of being in a dark theater with Drake sitting beside me was too appealing to turn down.

"Anything scary out?" I loved scary movies. The way the suspense made your heart race was incredible. Usually, I was the girl screaming, but I never covered my eyes to hide from the monster on the screen.

His eyes sparkled. "I'm sure we could find something scary."

Paranormal Activity 2 had me clutching Drake's arm throughout the movie. I screamed a few times, but I wasn't the only one. I felt safe with the big man seated next to me, his arm resting along the back of my chair and the popcorn sitting between us. It felt so good, so normal.

--

The weeks passed so quickly I didn't have time to really look at what was going on outside in the real world. Jesse and my sister were getting serious. Emmie's belly was getting even bigger. School was the same old shit over and over again.

What I had labeled as a crush was turning into something deeper, and it scared the hell out of me. Drake was becoming very important to me, and I didn't know how to handle it. All I did know was that I couldn't go two minutes without thinking about him. I felt like if I didn't see him every day, or get a dozen texts from him, I would go insane with this all-consuming love inside my heart. As hard as I tried to keep reminding myself that we were just friends, my heart refused to listen.

Layla threw Emmie a surprise baby shower, and it was a big success. Emmie, the hard-ass that normally took care of everyone else, was getting taken care of for a change, and she cried like the hormonal pregnant woman she was. It was a great day.

The next day Jesse loaded us up and took us to SeaWorld. The four of us felt like a family that day, and I felt like I could get used to it. Jesse was constantly holding Layla's hand and even carried Lucy on his shoulders when her feet got tired. The only thing that could have made the day better was if Drake had come with us.

But he had still been in bed when we left that morning. I wasn't blind to Drake's flaws. I knew that he was a heavy drinker. I wished he would find a way to give up his addiction. I wanted to be more important to him, special enough for him to give up the liquor for me, but I knew that that wasn't going to happen. I was just his friend—okay, I was likely his best friend—and it wasn't going to change.

The next weekend I got the surprise of my life when Drake pulled out all the stops and threw me a surprise birthday party. I was officially eighteen now, and there was no one I wanted to celebrate adulthood more with than Drake… His present on the other hand caused a mammoth fight.

The white Audi A6 was a dream car. It was also pretty expensive in my book. I didn't want to take it. Hadn't the stupid man realized that I didn't want him to buy me things like this? I almost refused it, but Emmie stepped in and made me feel like the biggest bitch that walked the earth. "It's yours. Your name is on the paper work. Take the car and stop tormenting him!"

I hadn't realized that I was tormenting him, but once she had said that I knew it was true. He only wanted the best for me. Layla's car had broken down more than once in the last three weeks. One of those times I had nearly been in an accident because the car had stalled in the middle of an intersection. The car was his way of keeping me safe.

I threw my arms around his neck and kissed his cheek. "Thanks for the car, Drake. I love it! Will you come with me while I test drive it?"

Just like that I was forgiven. He didn't even scold me when I got out on the highway and pushed the Audi to its limits. At one point I glanced over at him and he had the biggest grin on his face. When he smiled like that, his eyes glowed with pure unadulterated joy, and it took my breath away.

The following weekend all hell broke loose. Jesse took Layla to a party at a friend's Drake stayed home with me, and we made popcorn and watched a couple of movies. When I asked about their friend Tom and realized that Tom was Tommy Kirkman, I went a little ballistic.

"No!" I jumped up, already reaching for my keys. Lucy was asleep in the bedroom. I couldn't leave her alone. "Fuck!"

"Angel, what's the matter?" Drake demanded, concerned. No wonder, I was acting crazy.

"I have to get to Layla!" I had to get her the hell away from Tommy Kirkman. My sister was going to need me. "Can you stay with Lucy?"

Drake grabbed my arms, stopping me from running out the door. "What is the matter, Lana?"

Lana. He never called me Lana anymore. It was always Angel. I was his angel and that was the way I wanted it to stay. "Tommy Kirkman?" He nodded his head. "He's Layla's dad."

That was all he needed to know for the moment. He called Nik and told him to come over to stay with Lucy, and then he was dragging me to the Audi and pushing me into the passenger seat. Within minutes we were headed toward Beverly Hills. Then he was demanding answers. "Why didn't you tell me Tommy was Layla's father?"

"Because we don't talk about our dads. They are touchy subjects that neither one of us are willing to bring up. I had no idea that your friend Tom was Tommy." It was a nightmare that the guy that Drake had told me was the guy that had taken him and the band under his wing was the dirt bag that had fathered my sister.

"Who is your father, Angel?" Drake suddenly asked.

I closed my eyes. Sadly enough, Tommy Kirkman was just as bad as my own father. "I don't want to talk about it, Drake." I whispered.

"Angel..."

"He isn't important," I told him. "He didn't want me and I don't want him! Please, just don't make me talk about him."

Drake was quiet the rest of the drive into the Hills.

The rest of that night was crazy. Layla left the party with me and Drake, leaving Jesse behind. I was sure that Layla was going to pack us up and move. I could feel the tension building in Drake with each passing minute. A long while later, Jesse showed up beat all to hell. He had a bruised kidney, and the band ended up taking another week off from going into the studio.

40

Emmie scared us all the following Monday. Her water broke a week before her scheduled C-section, and she had to have an emergency C-section. Layla texted me from the hospital, and I left school to pick up Lucy. By the time I got there, the baby was already making herself known to the world!

I watched while the guys passed the little bundle of pink sweetness around. It was freaky to see all those big men with the tiny baby in their arms. They all stared down at her in wonder, and I could actually see their hearts getting tied to her. When Drake held her for the first time, I had to keep from crying. He was so careful with her, so lost in the moment of holding his little *niece*.

I had a mad moment of insanity and actually imagined him holding our baby like that one day. But I was only dreaming. No way was that going to happen. Drake made it clear and more clear every day that we were only friends.

41

Chapter 4

Drake

The addiction that I had for Lana and the peace she brought me escalated. Before I realized it was happening, I was spending every spare second with her. Sometimes I would have dinner with her and her sisters, or I would take her into the city and we would have a night out. At one point she even talked me into karaoke. Lana might look like an angel, but she didn't have the voice of one. I laughed until she punched me in the stomach when she sang *Girls Just Wanna Have Fun*.

The night of Tom's party was a bad night for me. Tom had been like a father figure to all of us, and that night I got to see just what kind of scumbag he really was. On top of that, I was terrified when I realized that Layla might leave. I didn't know if I could handle it if she took Lana away and I couldn't see her every day. To say I was relieved when she and Jesse made up was an understatement if I ever heard one.

Everyone was trying to prepare themselves for Emmie's C-section. The doctor asked all of us to come in and sat us down to explain what to expect the morning of the delivery. I thought I was ready. Really I did...

When she went into labor early and had to have an emergency C-section, I realized that no amount of planning would make me ready to see the fear in Emmie's eyes as the doctor prepped her for surgery. I just wanted to hold her until it was all over, but only Nik was allowed in the OR with her. Layla offered us all some comfort, rubbing my back as we waited for Nik to come out and tell us that Emmie was okay. It was soothing, but I wanted Lana there.

My angel didn't get to the hospital until it was almost time to see Emmie and the baby. When I saw her walking into the waiting room with Lucy beside her it felt like a weight had been lifted from my chest and I could breathe again. After tossing a greeting out to everyone, she sat down in the uncomfortable plastic chair next to me.

"Congratulations. You're an uncle!"

I laughed and pulled her close, brushing a kiss over her cheek. "I guess I am."

Holding Mia for the first time was a thrill in its own way. She was so tiny and I was terrified of dropping her. Lana showed me how to hold her head, and I had a moment of insanity and refused to even acknowledge the thought as soon as it flashed through my mind. When I saw her with that pink bundle in her arms, smiling down at my niece, I couldn't hide from it any more.

What would it be like to hold *our* child?

That was never going to happen! Lana was my friend, my *best* friend. When she had babies, I wasn't going to be their daddy...

That thought just made me pissed, and I left the hospital earlier than the others. I got lost in a bottle of Jack when I got home and stayed in my room for the rest of the night. I didn't want to think about Lana's future, especially if it included a husband and kids. That night as I fell into my nightmares, they were different. Instead of the past they were the future. I woke up in a pile of sweat just as Lana was walking down the aisle to some faceless prick.

I tried to pull back a little after that, but my resolve lasted about an hour before I felt like I couldn't breathe. Still, I tried to make it clear to Lana—and in turn clearer to myself—that we would only ever be friends. I could see that her feelings were growing for me, and I didn't want her to waste her time and have her fall for me when I wasn't good enough for her...

The week after Thanksgiving my feelings were shoved down my throat. I had to wake up quick to what was going on around me, especially when I walked into the guesthouse to find Layla packing. Her suitcase was sitting beside the door, and she had obviously been crying.

"What the fuck are you doing?" I exploded, unable to contain the fear that made my chest ache.

She shrugged. "Packing."

"No. No way." I shook my head, my hair falling into my face but I ignored it. "Where is Angel?" I demanded, glancing around for any sign of Lana. Jesse had pulled her outside with him, and I had figured that they were over here at the guesthouse.

"I thought she was with you."

"Jesse grabbed her and left. I figured she would be here." I glared at her. "Why are you packing, Layla? Why are you crying?"

"Because we are leaving." Her matter of fact tone had the blood draining from my face. "Look, you will still see Lana anytime you want. Just because we leave doesn't mean you have to stop being friends."

"No. You aren't leaving!" I shouted. "I can't... You can't..." I wasn't even making sense to myself let alone to her.

"Drake..." Layla started to say something, but I took a step back. This woman was about to take the best thing in my world away from me. I needed Lana and the peace she brought with her. I wouldn't survive without her.

The door opened and Lana walked in. Relief washed over me when I saw her. "You can't go, Angel!" I grasped her hands and held on tight. "Tell her!" I begged.

Her arms wrapped around me, and I buried my face in her neck. "Of course I'm not going anywhere," she whispered.

I pulled her to the couch and fell with her on my lap, keeping my face in her neck. The scent of her shampoo and lotion calmed me ever so slightly. Her fingers stroked over my jaw, making me hold on tighter. I couldn't let her go. No matter what, I needed her...

Oh, fuck! I was in love with her.

I loved Lana.

Not as just a friend, but I really loved her. It was new to me, and I was still determined that I wasn't going to touch her—at least not until she was older. In that terrifying instant I knew I was going to marry this girl. One day. She just needed time to grow up and experience the world a little more. And I would keep her safe until then.

"What are you doing, Layla?" Lana demanded quietly.

"Packing. We *are* moving, Lana. Tonight."

"Why? Why do we have to go?"

I tuned out Layla's answer. I didn't want to know why she was trying to take away my whole world. I might have even hated her right then. I didn't care if she was upset with Jesse. If she couldn't see how much my friend loved her, then that was her problem.

Lana jumped to her feet, and I missed her warmth. "Have you lost your mind?" she yelled at her sister. "Do you not see how much he loves you?"

"I know what I heard, Lana."

"You only think you do! Go talk to him. Let him explain."

"No, thank you. I've heard all I need to know."

Lana crouched down in front of me. "Drake, go get Jesse. Get Emmie too." She pulled me to my feet. "Tell them to hurry."

Knowing that if I didn't get Jesse to come fix whatever was broken with Layla, and Lana wouldn't be there come morning, I ran into the house and found Emmie in the living room with a cup of milk in her hands. She took one look at my face and grabbed me.

"Drake? What's the matter?" she demanded.

"Lana..." I shook my head, unable to form words with my heart beating so fast.

Emmie's eyes darkened. "Of course. It's always got something to do with Lana," she muttered. "I'll deal with it."

I didn't have time to correct her. Instead, I took the stairs three at a time. Jesse's bedroom door was closed; I didn't even knock as I barged in. He wasn't there, but the shower was running in the bathroom connected to his room. I didn't hesitate as I opened up the shower door. It wasn't the first time I had seen Jesse's junk, and it wouldn't be the last.

"Dude!" Jesse yelled.

"Layla's packing! She's going to leave."

"What?!" He was covered in soap but that didn't stop him from grabbing for a towel. He nearly fell on his ass as he ran past me, wrapping the towel around his waist.

With Jesse gone I was left alone in the steamy bathroom. The events of the past half hour started to catch up to me, and I suddenly felt as if I couldn't handle another second without a drink. I stumbled down the hall to my room and found my last fifth of Jack.

Lana

As soon as Jesse arrived, I knew that everything was going to be okay. Drake's reaction earlier had bothered me, and I wanted to go check on him. If he was this upset over me leaving Malibu, how would he react when I left for college? Emmie followed me out of the guesthouse, still in a huff because Layla had overreacted and thought the worst of both her and Jesse.

I stopped on the patio and turned to face her. "Why is it that every time Drake is upset you automatically assume it's my fault?" I asked.

She sighed. "Because since you came along, it is your fault when he's that upset." Green eyes glared at me. "You have the power to make him fall on his knees, Lana. I don't think you realize it, but sometimes I wonder if you do and you get off on making him hurt."

I blanched at her words. "I would do anything to keep him from hurting, Em," I whispered. "If you don't know that, then you don't know me."

Hurt by her words, I scrubbed at the tears that leaked from my eyes and hurried into the house. I looked all over the house, trying to find Drake. Finally, I climbed the stairs and knocked on his bedroom door. He didn't answer, but I could hear him moving around inside. Carefully, I opened the door.

He was sitting on the edge of his bed, a bottle of Jack Daniels in his hand. Fifteen minutes—tops—had passed since I had last seen him. I wasn't sure if the bottle had been opened before now or not, but it was halfway gone. His face was pale and his fingers trembled. I crossed to the bed and dropped down beside him. Drake didn't even raise his head.

"Are you okay?" I murmured.

"Getting there," he muttered, taking another chug from the bottle. Two more swallows and the bottle was empty. I grimaced as the bottle hit the floor and he fell back on the bed, one arm covering his eyes.

"Does that really help?" I couldn't stop myself from asking.

"It does a pretty good job. But, no, it doesn't really help." He sighed and lifted his arm from his eyes. "Is she still ready to leave?"

"I'm confident that once Jesse has talked to her she will be packing her bags for another reason." His face darkened and I sighed. "Jesse bought the house two houses over. He's going to ask my sister to marry him. I'm leaving, but I'm not going very far, Drake."

"Oh," he muttered.

I fell down beside of him, using his shoulder as a pillow for my head. "Are you drunk yet, Drake?"

"Yes and no. I shouldn't have drank that so fast. It's going to catch up to me soon." His arm wrapped around my waist. "I don't want you to go, Angel."

I smiled and leaned in to kiss his rough cheek. "I'm not going anywhere right now, babe."

Somehow, I managed to get us both turned right on the bed and under the covers. Drake had chugged the whiskey, leaving him half asleep, so I settled down to take a nap, not wanting to be anywhere but right here in his arms. Just before I closed my eyes, my cellphone buzzed, and I pulled it from my hip pocket to see that it was from Jesse.

She said yes! Do me a favor and stay in my room tonight. You don't want to come home. 🗆

I grinned, happy for my sister and Jesse.

Finally, I let myself drift off to sleep, safe in the arms of the man I loved...

Chapter 5
Lana

Something tickled my cheek. Without opening my eyes, I lifted my hand to brush it away. When I felt nothing, I tried to drift back to sleep.

The tickle came again, and I moved my hand quicker than before, but still came into contact with nothing. Sighing, I turned my face away, snuggling into a pillow that smelled like Drake. A smile teased my lips as I inhaled deeply, savoring the scent.

When a tickle to my other cheek came, I frowned and opened my eyes. Drake was propped up on an elbow, leaning over me while his long fingers caressed over my cheek.

"I thought you were never going to open those beautiful eyes," he murmured.

There was something different about Drake. I was sure that he was drunk, but he didn't talk like he was. His speech wasn't slurred and his movements weren't awkward. However, there was a glassiness in his eyes that told me he wasn't himself. At the moment, he was staring down at me with hunger in his blue-gray eyes.

I caught his fingers that were still caressing my cheek and linked our fingers together. "How are you feeling?"

"I feel as if I will lose my mind if I don't kiss you right now, Angel. That's how I feel." His voice was deeper, full of promises that I was sure he wouldn't have been offering if he were sober.

Maybe it was taking advantage, maybe it was being selfish, but I really didn't give a damn. I released his hand and wrapped my arms around his neck. "There isn't anything stopping you, Drake," I told him. "Kiss me."

"Is it what you want, Angel?" he asked, his eyes focused on my lips. "Is it what you really want?"

49

"I want you, Drake. It's all I will ever want," I promised him, letting my fingers comb through his unkempt hair.

My answer was all he needed. His dark head lowered. The first brush of warm lips against my own, how my heart stopped for just a second only to race the next, was a feeling I would never forget as long as I lived. My blood turned to lava as his tongue barely brushed over my bottom lip, and I felt like I was going to singe the sheets. My own tongue snuck out, and I got my first taste of Drake.

It was a mix of whiskey, cinnamon, and something more erotic. I couldn't put a label on it, but I knew that it was all Drake. That first taste was heady, and I instantly craved more of it. I opened my mouth, silently inviting him in to play so I could have more. The tip of his tongue tickled the roof of my mouth as he tangled it around my own.

A moan left me without my realizing it. My body was aching, my breasts swelling in the tight confines of my bra. I wanted it off, needed it gone, so that they wouldn't hurt so badly. Lower, I could feel my panties growing damp and tried to hide it by crossing my legs.

My movements caused his head to raise. "Okay?" His voice came out as a growl, almost animalistic.

I nodded. "Yeah." My own voice was all breathy. "Kiss me again."

He grinned that grin that only I could make appear. "Oh, I'm going to."

He brushed his nose with mine, and I felt his lips caressing my cheek. His lips were soft but firm. They trailed across my cheek to my jaw. Sharp teeth nipped at my ear lobe, making goose flesh pop up along my arms. My nipples, already aching in the now tight confines of my bra, pebbled.

My back arched, trying to find relief from the pleasure filled pain. Drake's hand cupped one breast, his strong fingers squeezing just hard enough to make me cry out. He didn't lift his head as he massaged my breast while his lips trailed down my neck, and he sucked at the spot where neck met shoulder.

"Your skin tastes so sweet." He bit down just hard enough to make me beg for more. "I want to eat you up."

I pushed at his shoulders until he lifted off of me a little. With some space between us, I sat up enough to reach behind me and undo the two clasps that fastened my bra. When the tight undergarment was undone, I let out a relieved sigh.

"Are you hurting, Angel?" he asked, and I nodded. "Come here. I'll make you feel better." He gripped the end of my shirt and stripped it off me in one smooth motion. My bra was hanging loosely, the straps halfway down my arms, the rosy pink color a nice compliment to the peaches and cream tone of my skin.

Drake's fingers were trembling ever so slightly as he pulled the satin material away, exposing my tits to him for the first time. I was proud of them. The full C-cups were perfectly rounded and didn't sag the way some bigger breasted women's tended to do. He raised his big hands and cupped both tits, my head swimming with desire.

His thumbs stroked over the hardened nipples. "Fuck, Angel. You are absolutely perfect."

"I'm glad you think so." I leaned into his touch, wanting more. "I'm aching, Drake. Please help me."

His eyes darkened making gold specks appear inside the irises. "Lie back," he commanded, and I fell back against his pillow. My breasts bounced as I landed, and he couldn't seem to draw in a breath as he watched them for a moment. I grasped his hands and pulled him toward me.

Instead of kissing me again, like I hoped he would, his head drifted lower. I wasn't prepared for his hot mouth engulfing my nipple. I cried his name and raked my fingers through his hair, holding him to me as he sucked roughly. Each suck caused muscles deep within my abdomen to contract, and my panties grew wetter by the minute. I could smell that wetness with each shallow breath I inhaled.

Drake's head rose and I started to protest, but he only switched from one breast to the other. My eyes rolled back in my head as he tugged the nipple with his teeth, biting down enough to make me breathe his name in either protest or encouragement; I wasn't sure which. He kissed the sting away and licked around the wide areola.

Unable to keep my hands still, I reached for his shirt and practically tore it off him in my haste to get his chest bare. It was free of tattoos, unlike his back, but his abs were defined, and I ran my fingers over the hard angles as he continued to shower kisses over both of my aching breasts.

His whole body trembled at my caressing touch. It was a powerful feeling, making a man tremble. I skimmed my fingers lower, circled his navel with my fingernail, and then kept going. I gripped the edge of his jeans and felt the top of his cock.

He jerked as if I had electrocuted him. His eyes found mine, and I knew that for him it was over. He was too far gone for this to go any slower than it already was, but I was more than ready to kick things into a higher gear. I was soaking wet and needed something I couldn't even describe. This was passion and no one but Drake could make me feel it.

My jeans and panties disappeared, as did Drake's jeans. He wasn't wearing anything underneath, and as soon as he unsnapped the top button, his cock sprung free. I watched as it swayed back and forth with each jerky movement he made to get his jeans off. When he was free of them, he dropped down beside me and pulled me across his chest.

I kissed him, took control of his mouth, and refused to relinquish my hold on it until I was half drunk on his intoxicating taste. I licked my way down his chest, fascinated by the way his flat nipples tightened as I raked my nails across them. His stomach muscles quivered as I licked each indention of his abs.

My hair was in my way. I pushed it out of my face and held it in place so I could raise my eyes and watch him as I kissed from his navel down to his groin. When I came to his cock, I took my time examining it. It stood proudly from the nest of dark curls. The tip was a dusky pink color and glistened with his pre-cum. Entranced by the sight of it, I rubbed my thumb over the wet head.

Drake made a growling sound in the back of his throat. "Angel..."

My eyes found his once more, and I slowly lowered my head until my tongue could touch the thick head of his cock. He gripped my hair tightly but didn't rush me. The taste of him exploded on my tongue, a mixture of musky and salty flavors that I wanted more of.

He pulled me away before I could take him fully into my mouth like I wanted to do. "No. I can't control myself if you do that."

"But I want to." I pouted.

"Later. Next time," he promised, and I relished in the knowledge that this wasn't going to end after tonight.

"Okay." I gave in. "Kiss me again."

"Whatever you want, Angel." He laid me down on the pillows. Eyes dark with passion looked down at me as he brushed a tender kiss over my lips, but he didn't linger.

Using his knees, he spread my thighs wide. Maybe I should have been embarrassed, but I wasn't. This was Drake, after all. How could I be embarrassed about anything I did with him? The way he was looking down at me, the way his eyes seemed to be soaking up the sight of the dampness on my thighs, only made me feel pride. He liked what he saw, the evidence both in his eyes and the way his cock twitched more and more with each passing second.

His fingers spread my outer lips, exposing my clit to him. The tip of his index finger carefully skimmed over it, and I whimpered from the sheer pleasure of it. My heart started racing more, my body melting more and more with each gentle brush of that one finger. Drake moved quickly, and before I could guess what he was doing, his mouth replaced his finger.

My entire body rippled with pleasure. My hips lifted of their own volition in an attempt to get closer to those pleasure inducing, talented lips. He sucked the hardened bundle of nerves into his mouth much like he had my nipple, making a popping sound each time he released it. I was on the edge of something dangerous, something so earth shaking that I knew I wasn't going to be the same when I fell.

"You're close, Angel," he told me. "Let go. I want to take you there." Even as he said the words, he pushed a finger inside of me. His finger fit tightly inside, and then he started stroking a spot deep inside that made it impossible to hold on a second longer...

Tears spilled from my eyes, my breathing coming in shallow little pants. When I was able to open my eyes after being momentarily blinded from the pleasure, I found Drake with his dick in his hand. He was stroking himself rapidly as he watched me come down from the high of my first orgasm.

I was jealous of his hand. I didn't want him pleasuring himself when I so desperately wanted to be touching him! "No," I told him in a voice rough with lingering desire. "I want you to come in me."

"I don't have anything, Angel. I don't have anything to protect you."

I bit my lip. "Do you need to?" Out of all the things we had talked about, I had never once asked him if he had any STDs. I never thought we would get this far, and it hadn't crossed my mind until right now.

"Only from getting pregnant," he told me. "I'm clean. I swear it."

Relief filled me and I pulled him down on top of me. "Then don't worry about protection. I want to feel you inside of me, Drake."

"Oh, fuck, Angel." He kissed me and I could actually taste myself on his lips. It was both erotic and arousing. "Are you sure?"

"I have never been surer of anything in my life," I assured him.

With gentle hands he spread my thighs wide once more. His big, beautiful cock was gripped in his hand, and he ran the head of it through my damp folds. With that one touch, it was like I hadn't just come apart for him. My body knew that he offered pleasure now, and it was greedy for more.

When the tip of his cock slipped into the place that no man had ever been, I was already half way there. Drake entered me an inch at a time until he met with resistance from my virginity. He stopped, eyes closed while he tried to draw in a breath. "So tight," he muttered almost to himself. "Can't hold on for long."

He felt so good inside of me, stretching me farther than his finger had only minutes ago. He didn't go any deeper, didn't move at all as he took my hand and brought my fingers to his lips. I watched in awe as he sucked the first two into his mouth until they were dripping wet. I had no clue what he was planning to do until he guided my fingers down to where we were connected.

When my soaked fingers touched my throbbing clit, it was like little rockets exploded deep inside of me. I was slick from my previous release, but the lubricant of his spit made the slip and slide of my fingers over that bundle of nerves that more erotic. Within a few minutes, I was hanging on the edge of a bone melting orgasm.

My inner muscles clenched and released with each rough caress as he continued to guide my hand. His jaw clenched tight as he waited for me to reach the point of no return. My breath was coming in hitched little pants, and I whimpered as he started to gently rock back and forth, stretching a little at a time with each movement of his hips.

"Oh, GOD!" I cried. "Drake...!"

The orgasm hit me. My thighs were trembling and my inner muscles seemed to be pulling him deeper. I wasn't sure if he meant to be so rough, or if he just couldn't hold back a second longer, but he thrust deep, breaking through my virginity and making me cry out in both pleasure and pain. My nails scraped down his back as I attempted to understand if I was hurting or dying from pleasure.

--

I slowly floated back into my body. My heart was still beating fast, but my breathing was trying to even out. Drake was lying heavily on top of me, but I savored the feeling of his sweaty body against my own.

His body was trembling, and I turned my head to find him staring down at me with tears in his eyes. My heart clenched.

"What's wrong?" I whispered, fighting tears of my own. I had no clue what was going through his head, but whatever it was couldn't have been good.

"I never want this moment to end," he murmured and kissed my lips. "I don't want the nightmares to creep in and take this dream away from me."

"Honey, this isn't a dream. I'm real." I returned his kiss just to prove it to him. "We were amazing together."

He rolled onto his side, taking me with him as he tucked me close. "I know. But as soon as I close my eyes, they will come."

My arms tightened around him. "Tell me about the nightmares," I urged. "Tell me what happened."

Drake was quiet for a long while, and I started to think that he had finally passed out when he surprised me by speaking.

"My stepdad did things," he said and blew out a long breath full of remembered pain and anger. "I thought it was just me, thought that Shane was safe from that sick prick. It wasn't until I was nineteen that I found out that I was wrong."

As he told me about his stepdad and the terrible things the monster had done to him, I listened, careful to not let what I was feeling show on my face or even by a quiver in my body. I was sickened, horrified that those things had happened to the man I loved. In no way did it make me love Drake less or want him any differently. I skimmed my fingers up and down his arm, offering comfort in the only way I knew he would let me.

"My mom killed herself," Drake told me, scrubbing his hand over his tear streaked face. "She shot Rusty with the cop's gun because no one expected her to grab for it. Two shots, right in the middle of his chest. Then before Shane or Nik or any of the cops could stop her...she turned it on herself."

A small sob escaped me, and I buried my face in his chest, aching for him. "I'm so sorry," I whispered.

His fingers stroked through my hair, soothing me when I should have been the one offering the comfort. "Don't cry, Angel." He kissed the top of my head. "She... She just couldn't handle that she had let the man that close to her sons. It destroyed something inside of her when Shane told her what had happened to him."

"I'm not crying for her. I'm crying for you," I told him as I continued to sob, unable to stop the tears. "You were all alone. In a way you still are, despite your brother, the band, and Emmie. You're all alone with your pain, and I want so much to be the one that helps you... That sounds selfish, I know, but it's true."

After a few more minutes of crying, I pulled away and lifted up onto my elbow. "I need a shower."

"Go ahead." He yawned. "I don't think I can keep my eyes open a minute longer."

57

When I came out of the bathroom ten minutes later, he was passed out. I used a warm washcloth to clean off the small traces of blood still on him from where he had torn through my virginity, and he didn't even move. Shaking my head at the way he had the pillow tucked under his chin I pulled on my panties and one of his tee shirts and crawled into bed beside him.

Chapter 6
Drake

I woke with a splitting headache and a sour stomach. Nothing unusual about that.

The girl snuggled up against my side, now that was a surprise. It took me a minute to realize that it was Lana and not some groupie. That was a relief...for about a second. Then I realized I was naked and Lana was only wearing my tee shirt.

I sat up in bed so fast my head and stomach protested at the same time. Lana protested beside me. "Drake, come back to bed," she murmured, yawning.

"Lana, wake up!" I shook her shoulders.

She blinked her eyes and I was assaulted by those hypnotic whiskey eyes. "Okay, okay. I'm awake." She pushed the hair out of her eyes. "What's wrong? It's Saturday and I want to sleep in."

"What happened last night?" I demanded, my tone coming out hard and cold. I didn't mean to do that, but I really needed to know if I had to apologize for something I might have done the night before. The last thing I remembered was Lana tucking the covers around us.

Now wide awake, she frowned. "You don't remember last night?" she asked with a frown. "Nothing?"

I shook my head. It wasn't unusual for me to not remember after chugging liquor like I had the night before. I blacked out when I did stupid shit like that. "No. Nothing. Did something happen?"

She stared up at me for what felt like an eternity, but I couldn't read anything in her eyes or expression. No emotion crossed that beautiful face. Finally, she gave me a smile, and I tried to pretend like I didn't notice it hadn't reached her eyes. "No, Drake. Nothing happened last night."

THE ROCKER THAT NEEDS ME

"Then why are you wearing my shirt?" I couldn't help but ask.

She shrugged. "I needed something to sleep in." She pushed the covers off and stood. With her back to me, she bent down and picked up her clothes. "I'm going to use your shower so the whole house doesn't freak out and assume something happened too," she called over her shoulder as she headed for the bathroom.

I sat on the edge of the bed, watching her until the door was closed. Her answer hadn't exactly set me at ease, and I searched for proof that something had happened. No damp spots on the sheets. The sheets didn't smell like sex. I fell back on the pillows, relieved. The first time I kissed, touched, made love to Lana I was going to be stone cold sober. If I had done that last night, it would have ruined everything. All the plans I had for our future would be destroyed.

I quickly got dressed and headed downstairs, wanting to give Lana her privacy. It wasn't lost on me that I had woken up without the sheets tangled and the place reeking of my fear and sweat. I couldn't remember any nightmares haunting me last night. It had to be because Lana had slept in my arms, and I wondered how I could get her to sleep there again without anything happening between the sheets.

I found Layla making breakfast, humming softly as she scrambled eggs and fried some steaks. My stomach growled as I poured myself a cup of Jesse's special coffee. "Morning, Layla," I greeted as I took my first sip of thick, bitter coffee.

She turned to me with a smile on her face that was bright enough to light the entire house. "Morning, Drake. Are you hungry?" She turned two of the steaks and then reached into the oven to check on the biscuits.

"Starving." I fell into a chair at the kitchen table. "You look happier than the last time I saw you. Things okay now?"

She turned with a pan full of hot biscuits. "I want to apologize to you for yesterday. I overreacted to something I heard and..." She sighed and shook her head. "I'm sorry I put you through that."

"Hey, baby!" Jesse walked into the kitchen in nothing more than a pair of jeans and a grin. "God, that smells good." He placed a kiss on her lips and reached for the coffee pot. "Morning, Dray. You ready for Vegas?"

I blinked, not sure I was following him. "What's happening in Vegas?" Were we doing a show that I had forgotten about?

"I asked Layla to marry me yesterday, and we don't want to wait. So we're all going to Vegas later." He swallowed his coffee and poured some more into his mug. "You gotta come, man. I need you all there."

I grinned. "I wouldn't miss it for the world, bro." I assured him. He had no idea how happy he had made me. If he was marrying Layla, then Lana would be around for a long, long time.

I was just digging into my steak and eggs when Shane came into the kitchen. He was sweating from his run, but he was grinning. I wasn't sure if it was because he was happy for Jesse or if he was excited about getting to go to Vegas for the weekend. More than likely it was the latter. There was too much shit he could get into, and he was ready for it all.

"Dude, I can't believe you're getting married and we don't get to do the bachelor party thing. I've been looking forward to this since Layla whipped your ass into saying you love her." Jesse gave him a glare, but Shane pretended not to notice. "Come on, man. Give us tonight and you can marry her in the morning."

"No. I'm not spending another night without her as my wife. You fuckers can go out and pretend I'm hiding in the bathroom or something." Jesse tossed a biscuit at Shane's head. "Leave me out of it."

"It won't be any fun without you," Shane whined. "You know Nik won't join us, and Drake doesn't do parties anymore."

"Poor little thing." Layla laughed. "I'm sure you can find some kind of debauchery to get into on your own. It's Vegas, the City of Sin. Sin and Shane go hand in hand."

I rolled my eyes at my brother. "I'll go with you."

"Really?" Shane looked excited again. "You won't bail on me for Lana?"

"I promise." I guess I had been doing just that lately. Maybe Shane and I needed some quality brother time. Of course, when it came to my brother that usually meant strippers or hookers, or something else that involved women with as few clothes as possible.

Lana

As soon as Lucy was home from her sleepover, we all packed the Escalade. It had room for seven, but with the baby's seat and three extra people, Shane decided to take his car too. Despite the rocky start to my morning, I climbed in the cramped backseat of the disgustingly expensive, sex on wheels car.

With Shane behind the wheel and Drake riding shotgun, I wondered if I would make it to Vegas in one piece. Still, they had me laughing, and the five hour trip seemed to fly by. We pulled up to the hotel, jamming to some rock music that I had gotten to like over the last five hours. Shane had insisted on listening to the same songs over and over again until I knew every song by heart.

Nik pulled in behind us just as a valet took Shane's keys. Emmie, efficient as always, had us checked in and in our rooms in less than fifteen minutes. Jesse and Layla got the honeymoon suite on the top floor while the rest of us were on the same floor. Drake took the room next to mine and Lucy's, and Shane opted for the one at the end of the hall. Nik and Emmie got the one a few rooms over.

I loved our room. Lucy, hyped up from having to spend so long in a vehicle, was jumping on one of the queen sized beds while I took a minute to look out the window at the Strip. It was beautiful in the evening light, and I couldn't help but stare down at it in wonder.

A connecting door led into Drake's room, and I knocked twice before he answered. He had a tooth brush in his hand, probably to get the taste of Red Bull out of his mouth since he and his brother had chugged several each on the drive.

"Hey, neighbor." I grinned up at him as I made myself at home in his room, which was an exact copy of my own except his bed was a king where mine had two queens.

"You should be getting ready," he called from the bathroom where he was rinsing out his mouth. "Aren't you supposed to be meeting Layla and Em downstairs to go dress shopping?"

I sighed. "Are you trying to get rid of me, Drake?"

"Of course not. I just don't want you to keep the bride waiting." He stuck his head out of the bathroom. "You seriously need a nap, Angel. You're starting to sound like a cranky bitch. It started just outside of the Nevada state line."

I gave him the finger and turned toward my room. "Nice. I'll talk to you later, asshole."

Strong arms wrapped around my waist before I could reach the door. "Don't leave mad," he murmured against my ear. My shiver was involuntary, making my entire body come alive. "I'm sorry I called you a bitch..." he kissed the back of my head "...but you have been cranky."

I closed my eyes. He was right. I had been cranky. The events from the night before and this morning kept replaying in my head, and I wanted to hit something. I had been stupid and now I was paying for that stupidity.

"You're right. I'm sorry." I leaned into him for another few seconds before pulling away. "I'll try to do better," I promised, shooting him a forced smile over my shoulder.

Lucy and I met Layla and Emmie downstairs. There was plenty of time to shop for dresses since Layla wasn't looking for the typical wedding dress. "Just something beautiful," was her only requirement.

Emmie, having been to Vegas a few times, knew some really good boutiques that didn't cater to the trashy and nasty. We all found something pretty to wear, except for Lucy. She required an additional stop. I loved Emmie's silver dress. It ended about mid-thigh and showed off her milk filled breasts beautifully. My own was a shimmery blue that was a little more conservative in length but just as daring at the bust. I had them and tonight I wanted to make sure that Drake realized I had them too.

Nothing compared to Layla's dress. It was creamy beige and hugged her curves, letting everyone see her for the goddess she was. The sheer happiness shining from her big chocolate brown eyes made my breath catch when I saw her after we had all showered and gotten dressed.

A car was waiting for us down stairs. Lucy tugged at her blue lacy dress, not used to wearing a dress at all. "You two look beautiful," Layla murmured as the car pulled into traffic.

"Not nearly as beautiful as you, Layla," I assured her, blinking back tears. "I'm so glad you're happy. No one deserves it more than you."

"Stop it," Emmie scolded gently. "Don't you two dare start crying! It took me forever to get my makeup just right." But she was already blinking rapidly, tears filling those big green eyes of hers. Mia cooed between us, letting us know that she wanted in on the conversation too. It broke the serious moment and we all laughed, wiping away the tears that had escaped. Before I knew it, the car was pulling to a stop outside an adorable little chapel.

It was white, and more serious than some of the other chapels in Vegas. The man and woman that ran it had been married for fifty-two years and only married people they deemed truly in love. If they couldn't see how in love Layla and Jesse were, then they were blind.

Emmie left us in the back of the chapel for a few minutes while she made sure everything was perfect. When she returned she was without the baby and all smiles. "Okay. How would you like to do this Layla? Do you want one of the guys to give you away?"

She bit her lip and glanced from me to Lucy. "No. I think Lana and Lucy should walk me down the aisle. We kind of come as a full package anyway." She blinked, fighting tears again. "Will you give me away, girls?"

"Of course we will, silly." I kissed her cheek, careful not to mess up our makeup.

With Emmie leading the way as the matron-of-honor, we walked Layla down the aisle. As we started the short walk, I looked at the front of the chapel. Jesse was all smiles at Layla, the same light shining from his unusual, ever changing eyes.

Beside him stood all three of his band brothers: Nik, Drake, and Shane. I couldn't help but linger on Drake as my eyes took them all in. Their suits looked new and they probably were. Drake Stevenson looked hot as hell in a pair of ragged jeans and a thread bare tee shirt, but in a suit that looked like it was made just for him? Oh dear Heaven above!

As Lucy and I handed our sister over to Jesse Thornton's safe keeping for eternity, I was unable to keep my tears at bay a second longer. My sister was so happy she was trembling. Jesse's fingers actually shook as I put my sister's hand in his. The owner's wife discreetly offered me a tissue as I took my place behind Emmie, and I dabbed at my damp eyes.

By the time Layla had said, "I do," Emmie and I were both quietly sobbing. The owner's wife tossed rose petals at the happy couple as they walked back down the aisle. I started to follow after them when Emmie rushed into Nik's arms, sobbing.

"I'm sorry! I'm so sorry. I love you. I want to get married."

65

"Ah, Em!" Jesse called from the front of the church. "Couldn't you have waited a day or so longer?" But he was grinning.

Emmie shook her head. "I don't want to get married in Vegas. I want to do it right...Not that this isn't awesome, Layla," she was quick to correct, "but I want a small wedding back at the house..." She looked up at Nik with hope in her big green eyes. "Will you marry me, Nik?"

He laughed, his ice blue eyes glazed with tears. "Yes, Emmie. I will marry you."

--

Lucy was exhausted by the time I carried her up to our room. After the wedding we had gone out for dinner and Emmie had pulled out all stops to get us the VIP room at one of the most exclusive restaurants in all of Las Vegas. There had been a full buffet waiting on us as well as a two tiered cake.

I hated to admit it, but Emmie could probably rule the world with her cell phone in hand if she wanted to.

After dinner, Nik and Drake sang one of the band's new songs as Layla and Jesse shared their first dance as husband and wife. I spent more time watching the way Drake's fingers strummed across the strings of the acoustic guitar, mesmerized as he played so effortlessly. And his voice! Good heavens his voice made something deep inside of me melt.

From the first time I had heard him sing, I had wondered why he wasn't the band's frontrunner. He just shook his head and told me that he didn't like being front and center on stage. He liked playing from the sidelines.

When Lucy had fallen asleep at the dinner table, I knew it was time to call it a night. Layla and Jesse had taken off for their honeymoon suite more than an hour before and Emmie and Nik were making noises about following. I had hoped that Drake would come up with me, but he had promised Shane a night on the Strip. So with a heavy heart, I had picked up my sleeping sister and carried her up to our room.

After tucking Lucy into her bed, I showered and sat on my bed flipping through channels. Before long, I was yawning and unable to keep my eyes open...

A noise startled me awake. At first I didn't know where the noise had come from. A glance over at the other bed told me that it hadn't been Lucy because she was still fast asleep. The television was turned down low, so it hadn't come from there...

A thumping against the wall made me jump, and I tossed back the covers. It had come from Drake's room next door, and I was scared something had happened to him. But when I raised my hand to knock on the connecting door, a moan caught my attention.

The moan hadn't come from Drake. It wasn't deep and rough, but high and feminine. I held my breath as I leaned in closer, trying to hear better even as my stomach rolled. When the moan came again, louder this time, I knew that they were just on the other side of the door. Another thump and the door vibrated as if someone was pushed up against it.

Tears burned my eyes and bile rose in the back of my throat as I heard the woman moan again and then...Drake's hoarse growl! I knew what was happening. The only thing that separated me from Drake fucking some random girl was a door three inches thick.

A sob escaped me and I ran for the bathroom, unable to listen a second longer as the woman's moans grew louder as her ecstasy increased with each passing second. I shut the door and turned on the shower, trying to drown out the sounds coming from the connecting hotel room.

I wasn't sure how long I sat there on the edge of the bathtub. All I was wearing was a pair of boy shorts and a tee shirt—ironically enough the same one I had slept in the night before because I had needed something of Drake's touching me while I slept. Now I was cold, the steam from the shower not providing enough heat to warm the coldness that had invaded my very soul.

My back began to ache from sitting like that for so long, and I slipped onto the floor, using the tub for support as I pulled my legs to my chest and rested my forehead on my knees as the tears continued to fall.

Sometime much, much later, my tears finally started to dry and the cold that had numbed me started to thaw enough to make me realize that I should be mad. I was in love with Drake, and after Friday night, I was sure that he was in love with me too, or that he at least cared about me as more than a friend... Now, with him fucking some other girl in his hotel room, unconcerned that I would hear him, I knew that I had been wrong.

All I would ever be to him was his friend, and I would have to accept that. But there was no way I could carry on the way we had been the last few months. I wasn't that good of an actress. I sucked at pretending, especially when my feelings were involved. And they didn't get any more involved than they were right now.

It would kill me to have to see him day after day, knowing that he had gone from lying in bed with me one night to screwing some other chick the next. Maybe that was how it worked in the rocker world—okay, so I knew that that *was* how it worked in the rocker world, but I couldn't deal with that kind of messed up shit.

As the night dragged on, I realized what I had to do. It was going to be hard. It meant doing things I had promised never to do, but sometimes you had to do what was best for you, not what was best for someone else.

With that thought firmly in mind, I stood and turned off the shower. When I entered the bedroom all I could hear was the voices coming from the television and sank down on the edge of my bed. Sleep eluded me. There was no way I could sleep now. Not without the sounds of the couple in the next room haunting me.

Chapter 7
Drake

There was a pounding in my head. I blinked open my eyes and frowned at the ceiling, unsure of where I was for a moment. When it came to me, I groaned and turned over in bed, determined to get a few more hours of much needed sleep.

"Drake!" Shane's voice called from the hallway as he pounded on my hotel room door. "Emmie said to get up, bro. We leave in half an hour."

I muttered a curse and scrubbed a hand over my stubble roughened jaw. "Dude, you drove. Why can't we wait until later?"

"Because I'm leaving the car for Jesse," Shane yelled through the door. "Now get your ass up!"

Still muttering curses, I stumbled into the bathroom and turned the shower on full blast. I smelled like smoke and booze and perfume. Damn Shane, wanting to go clubbing! I was pretty sure that I had brought a girl back with me last night, but couldn't remember her name or even what she looked like. She was already gone which told me all I really needed to know. She had been a groupie looking for a night in a rock star's bed.

Disgusted with myself, I scrubbed until my skin ached and then got dressed. I only had to toss a few things into my case and I was ready to roll.

Downstairs, I found everyone already loaded up. Jesse and Layla were staying for a week as a kind of honeymoon and would drive Shane's car back. So of course we all had to get into the Escalade. The only seat not taken already was the front passenger seat. Lucy and Lana had taken the smaller back seat with Emmie, Mia, and Shane in the middle one. I glanced back to check on Lana, but she had her head leaned against the window and her eyes were closed.

"Did you get everything?" Emmie asked as she tucked Mia into her car seat.

"Yeah, I made sure I packed everything." She was such a mother hen sometimes, but I didn't know what I would do without her.

"Then let's go." Emmie grimaced. "I have things to do when we get home."

Lana

How I made it through saying goodbye to my sister I will never truly know. Somehow, I was able to put on a smile and keep it on while she hugged me and Lucy. To my surprise, it was Jesse that saw through my façade and took me aside for a private talk.

"What's up?" he asked, his unusual eyes scanning my face. "You have circles under your eyes, and you're as pale as a ghost."

I avoided his eyes, trying to push my emotions down when they threatened to surface. "I'm fine. I stayed up all night watching television when I should have been sleeping."

"Liar," he accused.

I glared up at my new brother-in-law. "Look, I don't want to talk about it. Especially now. I don't want Layla to worry when she should be having a good time with you on your honeymoon."

He clenched his jaw, wanting to argue with me but unable to do so. He didn't want to upset Layla anymore than I did. "We are going to talk about it as soon as I get home. Understand?" I nodded. "Good. Until then, if you need anything let Emmie know...And make sure you take care of the college issue this week, Lana. I expect your decision when we get home."

Again, I nodded. I had already made my decision. It had been all I had thought about once I had fallen onto my bed in the early hours of the morning. For the first time in my life, I was willing to let someone buy me something expensive. A college education wasn't something that I was going to turn down, and it was my way of escaping which made it all the more appealing.

When we all piled into the Escalade, I was relieved to find myself in the very back. When Shane and Emmie took up the middle row, I pressed my head against the cool glass of the window and closed my eyes, thankful that I wouldn't have to be so close to Drake for the next five hours. When he finally slid into the front passenger seat, Nik pulled out into traffic and the long trip home began.

Everyone was quiet around me. Lucy was playing with her iPad while everyone else was doing what I was pretending to do. Drake's snores made me glance up at one point to see him fast asleep. Shane muttered something under his breath about waking the dead, and I felt the slightest of smiles tease at my lips.

Emmie, seeing that I was awake turned in her seat enough to face me. "Jesse said that you will have an answer this week," she whispered so she wouldn't wake the baby.

I nodded, my eyes still on Drake. "I'd like to talk to you about it when we get home, actually."

"Good. I can start the paperwork in the morning and get everything paid on time." She smiled. "I'm really excited for you, Lana."

Three bathroom stops and six miserable hours later, Nik pulled into the driveway in Malibu. As soon as my feet touched the ground, I grabbed my stuff and pulled Lucy toward the guest house. Emmie was going to have the new house decorated this week so we could be moved in by the weekend. Until then, I was sticking to the guesthouse.

"I'll carry your cases in, Angel," Drake called after me.

"Yeah, sure. Thanks." I pushed Lucy faster. As soon as I had her settled, I grabbed the two piles of paper work that I had narrowed down from twelve the week before and rushed into the main house.

Emmie was pulling a bottle of water from the fridge when I found her. Something in my expression must have told her that she wasn't going to like what I was going to do, but she didn't say anything as she led me down the hall to her office and closed the door. "Sit down, Lana." She sighed. "I have a feeling I'm going to need a drink after this," she said half under her breath.

I had narrowed my choices down to two schools. Both had everything I wanted in a college. UCLA would have been my first choice—had been my first choice up until the night before. So I tore up the acceptance letter and handed over the one that was about to change my life.

Emmie muttered a curse when she looked down at the letter and the packet that had come with it. Green eyes flashed fire as she met my gaze. "Why?" she demanded.

"Because it's where I need to be," I whispered.

"You need to be here, close to everyone that loves you. Layla is going to go ape-shit over this, Lana!" She stood, glaring down at the packet that contained all the paper work she would have to deal with come morning. "Have you even thought this through? What will you do that far away? You will be all alone in a big city. No Layla, no Drake..." She broke off when she saw me flinch at the mention of his name. "Is this about Drake?"

I looked away. "I *have* thought this through, Em. In fact, I have done nothing but think about it since about three o'clock this morning. Around the time the girl that Drake brought to his hotel room had left."

Emmie muttered something vicious and dropped down into her chair once more. "Lana, I know that your feelings run deep for Drake. But, honey, you two are just friends. He is going to screw around from time to time."

I met her gaze. "Like Nik screwed around while you two were just friends?" She flinched and I nodded. "How did that feel, Em? How did it feel knowing that the man you were in love with was off fucking someone else?"

Her green eyes darkened, and I was sure that I was going to get an earful because really that had been a bitch move. Instead, Emmie only nodded after a long pause. "Touché," she said. "I understand where you are coming from, but..."

"No buts!" I cried. "He was fucking her against the door that separated our rooms. I heard her moaning. I had to listen while he..." Tears scalded my cheeks, and I quickly wiped them away. "Maybe you think that I'm being a coward for running away, but right now I really don't give a flying fuck. I'm not as strong as you! I can't do this and not crack. I can't stay here and pretend that he didn't shatter my heart last night."

Emmie sat there, just looking at me. I didn't know what was going through her head, but I was sure she was trying to come up with something to excuse Drake's behavior the night before. Maybe it would have made me stop and rethink my decision. Maybe I would have listened and not make her put everything into motion so I could leave as soon as possible.

But then again, she didn't know about Friday night...

"Okay." Emmie surprised me by giving in without any more arguments. "I'll start on it first thing tomorrow. I'll get your dorm taken care of, set you up an allowance like Jesse said to, and maybe I can pull some strings and get you moved in early. Maybe some time away will put everything into perspective for everyone."

I let out a relieved sigh. If Emmie was on board, then I knew that Jesse wouldn't argue about my choice.

"But promise me something, Lana," Emmie said after a moment. "Promise me that it's only for one semester. Take this time away and get yourself pulled together. Then when summer starts, you come home. UCLA was what Jesse was hoping you would pick. It won't take much to get you into the fall semester."

I gave in and made the promise, but I wasn't sure if I would be able to keep it. I didn't know how Emmie expected me to "pull myself together" when my heart was in a billion pieces.

Chapter 8
Drake
Lana was avoiding me.

I knew that she had to study. She only had two more weeks of school left and her exams took up an entire week of that, but she didn't have time to text me back or have dinner with me. I had no idea what was up with her, and it was driving me up the wall.

It didn't actually bother me until one night midway through the week. Shane went out for his run and came back with Lana. They were walking, both of them sweating like they had run a marathon. I watched from the living room as Shane stopped on the patio and said something to her that made her chin tremble. My brother pulled her into his arms and hugged her.

Okay, I'll admit it. I wanted to punch my brother at that moment. His relationship with Lana was a strictly friends-in-passing kind of thing. They had only ever hung out when I was around. Now, all of a sudden, he felt like he could hug her...

Yeah, I was thinking of punching him, possibly in the throat or his pretty face that got him laid at least once a day.

I contained that urge, albeit with some difficulty. After all, it was a one-time thing. She was probably having an emotional melt down because she was working so hard studying. It wouldn't be the first time she cried because the stress of studying for a test became too much and she needed some kind of release before it drove her over the edge.

So I sucked it up and went to bed with a fifth of Jack.

The next night Lana went for a run with Shane again, and then again on Friday night before Shane went out. Apparently, she had time to go on an hour long run, but not enough time to eat with me. I was positive then that she was avoiding me on purpose, and I was determined to get to the bottom of it.

This week had sucked without her. There was no reason to smile when she wasn't around. No peace to be found when I didn't have her close. Before I passed out every night, it was with her name on my lips. When I woke every morning, just before the memories of the nightmares invaded my mind, and I went rushing for the toilet, it was her face that I saw behind my eyelids.

Saturday morning, I was determined to corner Lana and find out what was going on. I walked downstairs, dressed for the day, in hopes of talking Lana into going shopping with me. Christmas was only two weeks away, and I hadn't bought any presents yet. This was going to be the first year that we had an actual home to celebrate in, and I wanted to make it memorable.

As I got to the bottom of the stairs, I heard Jesse shouting from the back of the house. He and Layla must have left Vegas at the crack of dawn to get home so early. I was glad he was home. Maybe he could tell me what was going on with Lana.

"I don't want this!" he shouted. "Layla is going to go off the wall when she finds out." The door to Emmie's office slammed and Jesse came stomping down the hall.

"Hey, how was the honeymoon?" I asked when I saw him. His eyes narrowed on me, but he didn't answer as he stormed out of the house—typical Jesse behavior when he was in a rage. He probably hadn't even heard a word I said.

I opened my texts and sent Lana a quick message while I ate a bowl of cereal. The house no longer smelled like bacon morning, noon, and night, and I was starting to miss the smell if not the taste of fried pig.

By the time I had rinsed my bowl, Lana still hadn't texted me back. Clenching my jaw, I went in search of her. If she was pissed at me, she needed to tell me so I could fix whatever I had done. When I opened the door to the guesthouse, it was empty of their things. Everything was either at the new house or in storage.

77

Muttering a curse, I jogged down the beach to Jesse's house and knocked on the back door. Lucy opened it, a slice of toast sticking out from her mouth as she let me in. "Where is everyone?" I asked when I didn't see anyone else.

Lucy sighed. "They're upstairs. Lana's in trouble."

My eyebrows rose at that. "Why?"

"I don't know." She tossed the crust of her toast in the trash and reached for her glass of juice. "Jesse came in a little while ago. He started yelling, but I couldn't make sense of it. Layla started crying, and Lana ran upstairs. They've been up there for a few minutes now."

What the fuck was going on with Lana?

I took the back stairs up to the second floor. I had no idea which room was Lana's but Jesse's deep voice was coming from the one at the end of the hall, so I figured that was it. As I grew closer, their conversation was easier to hear behind the closed door.

"...something happened in Vegas." Jesse was saying. "I know it did. You were fine up until then."

"I don't want to talk about it," Lana told him. "Why can't you just accept that I want to go? You promised me that I could go to the college of my choice. Well, I chose this one!"

"You're running away!" Jesse shouted. "I know you, Lana. You wouldn't move all the way across the country for some fucking school unless you were running away from something. I thought you were smarter than this!"

"Jesse, that's enough," Layla's calmer voice interceded. "This is her choice. We have to accept that. She's eighteen, an adult. Whatever her reasons, she feels like she has to do this. I...I don't like it, but she knows what is best for her."

"Best for her? Being away from everyone that loves her? What if something happens?"

I couldn't take it a second longer. I turned the knob on the bedroom door and pushed it open. Lana stood by the window, her face streaked with tears. When she saw me, she paled. I watched her, startled when what felt like an invisible wall went up between us as she clenched her jaw and turned her head away so I couldn't see her face.

"Drake..." Jesse was standing by the dresser, a mixture of emotions on my band brother's face.

"I need to talk to Lana," I told him, knowing that I had interrupted a family situation but not giving a fuck.

Jesse stared at me for a long moment and then ran a hand over his face and smooth head. "I had so many plans for today. Nowhere was *this* part of them. I don't know what the fuck has been going on around here, but I've come home to a shit load of trouble that I am powerless to fix."

Layla put a hand on her husband's arm. "It's going to be okay. Really." She tugged on his hand, pulling him toward the door. As she passed me, she offered a small smile. "Good luck," she murmured and closed the door behind her.

I waited until their footsteps had faded before turning my eyes back to Lana. She was looking out the window, but I doubt that she was really seeing anything. "Are you mad at me?" I finally asked.

She bit her lip and shook her head. "No," her voice was clogged with tears.

I took two steps toward her but stopped when she looked at me. "Then why have you avoided me all week?"

"Because it's hard enough being this close to you without breaking apart." A tear escaped the corner of her left eye and spilled down her cheek.

"What does that mean?" I demanded, feeling like I was losing her right before my eyes, and I didn't even know why.

Lana slowly turned her head and met my gaze. "It means that I love you, Drake. And I know that I'm not supposed to. All you want from me is to be your friend. And I am, but I can't turn off my emotions. I can't hide how I feel. I've tried."

Her confession gutted me. I knew that her feelings were strong for me, but I had just brushed it off as a teenaged

79

infatuation. Now, I could see the truth shining at me from those whiskey eyes. Lana loved me.

My heart jumped for joy in my chest. That was all I had ever wanted, and I hadn't really realized it until this moment. "Lana..." I started to tell her I loved her too, but she went on.

"Maybe I could have kept hiding my love for you. I don't know. But last Saturday night showed me that I couldn't keep hiding it. I can't be just your friend anymore. Especially..." She closed her eyes, swallowing hard. "You brought a girl back to the hotel with you, and I realized that I can't keep doing this and keep all of myself intact."

I felt the blood drain from my face. Lana knew about the one-night stand in Vegas...Oh fuck. Our rooms had had connecting doors! Of course she would have known. She probably heard the whole damned thing. Nausea rolled in my stomach as I realized that I had no one to blame but myself.

"I'm sorry, Angel," I whispered. "I was drunk..." I knew being drunk didn't excuse any of it, yet drinking had always been my excuse. Now I was going to lose my best friend...

"I know, Drake," Lana murmured. "I know that you were drunk. And I know that you probably don't remember much from that night." Something flashed across her face, but I couldn't read the emotions in her eyes. "I still love you anyway. I wish I didn't. I wish I could turn it off and continue being just your friend...but I can't and that kills me."

I felt my eyes burn with tears. "Angel..."

"Remember that I told you about the early acceptances? Jesse promised me that I could go anywhere I wanted, and I was still undecided before he married my sister. But..." she swiped at the tears on her cheeks "...but I realized as I tried to drown out the sound of your moans as you... I realized that I couldn't stay here."

I went numb. I didn't feel the blow as Lana said she was going to NYU. I wasn't sure how deep the cut went, but I knew that when the numbness wore off it would be deep enough that I'd bleed to death. Three thousand miles. My angel was moving three thousand miles away from me, and it was all my fault...

Lana

I was miserable all week as I waited for my sister to come home from her honeymoon. I buried myself in studying, taking care of Lucy, and anything else that kept my mind off of Drake and the many texts he had sent.

Wednesday, I couldn't take being in the guesthouse a minute longer. For the first time in two years, I put on a pair of sweats and my running shoes. I had been on the track team back at my old school before my mother had died. It had been a requirement that everyone pick an after school sport, but I had loved track. Running had been my outlet to clear my mind when things were so bad at home.

I took solace in it again.

Lucy was asleep on our shared bed as I shut the front door behind me. I headed down the beach, determined to keep all thoughts of Drake out of my head, but it was no use. With every step I took, he was all I could think about. All our time together, all the fun we had shared together, even the arguments replayed in my head.

I ran faster, trying to excise him from my mind by putting unused muscles through a brutal workout. Two miles later, I was out of breath and lying on the beach, staring up at the night sky. Sweat soaked through my shirt and made the cool night air a little uncomfortable, but I welcomed it. The stars above mocked me, and I let the tears fall freely.

I didn't notice the other runner until he was almost over top of me. Shane stopped with his hands on his knees as he looked down at me. "Lana?"

I sighed. "Hey, Shane."

He dropped down beside me without asking if I wanted company, which I didn't. "Are you crying, Lana?"

"Looks like it," I muttered, sitting up and dusting the sand off my back. I had some in my hair, but I didn't care. Right now, I didn't give a flying fuck about anything.

"Did you and Drake have another fight?" he asked, both amused and concerned.

I shook my head, my eyes focused on the waves as the surf hit the beach. "I haven't seen your brother since Sunday." I had been able to avoid him but knew that my luck was running out. When Jesse and Layla got home, everyone would know what I had done. There was no way Drake wouldn't hunt me down then.

"Okay, you don't want to talk about it." Shane nodded. "I can understand that. Just know that if you need a shoulder, I have two strong ones to lean on."

"Yeah, thanks."

I had hoped that he would get up and continue with his run. Instead, he just sat there with me for the next hour. Neither of us spoke, not a sound uttered, but for some reason it eased some of the pain around my heart. Maybe it was because he was Drake's brother. We both loved Drake, after all. Or maybe it was just because Shane was Shane.

"I love him," I whispered, not sure why I was confessing my feelings.

"Yeah, I know."

"But he doesn't love me. Not the way I want."

"I don't know. Drake keeps a part of himself closed off, a part that not even I can reach, but I know that he does care about you, Lana." He draped his arm across my shoulders. "Especially after Friday night... Sorry, I heard you guys when I came home..."

I blushed. "He doesn't remember."

"Yeah, I figured." He grimaced. "I guess Saturday night was hard for you. I'm sorry, Lana. I shouldn't have taken him out with me. Maybe..."

"No. It wasn't your fault. It's no one's fault. Drake didn't really do anything wrong. I'm not his girlfriend. He's free to screw anyone he wants." That didn't mean I had to stick around to witness it.

"I'm still sorry. This can't be easy for you. Have you talked to him at all?"

I shrugged. "A text or two."

We were quiet for a while longer. It was getting late, but I wasn't sure I could sleep. Shane stood and offered me his hand. "Come on, sweetheart. You have school in the morning."

We walked side by side back toward home. A mile from the house, I confessed what I had done. Shane stopped, his face a mixture of emotions that I couldn't decipher in the moonlight. "Lana..."

I bit my lip. "I have to do this, Shane. I know it's going to hurt him, but right now I have to do what is best for me. That must sound selfish, and I'm sorry."

After a long pause he finally nodded. "Yeah, I understand."

He walked with me to the patio and asked if I wanted to go for a run with him the next evening. I knew he was just being nice, but I really needed someone right then. My chin trembled and I nodded. Shane sighed and pulled me into his arms. "It's going to be okay, Lana. Everything will work itself out."

Our run Thursday night was almost relaxing, and it left me looking forward to Friday evening since he had asked me to run with him again. After the stress of the last week, the running helped me relax, and I ended up falling into a deep sleep for the first time Friday night.

Saturday wasn't pretty. Layla was home earlier than I expected, and Jesse was already talking to Emmie about my college plans since she had left him a message that she needed to talk to him about it as soon as he got back. I wanted to be mad at her when Jesse stormed into the new house with rage in his eyes, but I couldn't. She was just looking out for Jesse after all.

"Lana, why?" Layla demanded, tears in her eyes as she turned to confront me. "I don't understand why you would do this."

With Jesse shouting and Layla crying, I couldn't handle the situation like I had wanted to. Unable to deal with it, I ran up to my new room. Of course Jesse followed me, wanting answers, and Layla joined the party, trying to diffuse the tension but wanting answers too. I could see that my sister suspected the truth; it was there in her eyes. She couldn't possibly know all of it, but she could guess, and knowing her, she would guess right.

I wasn't ready to face Drake when he stormed into my room. I wasn't ready for any of it, actually. Confessing everything—that I loved him, that I had heard him having sex against the hotel room door—hadn't been part of my plan, but I had to tell him. He deserved to know where I stood. That even though he had shattered my heart, I still loved him. *Would always love him.*

It nearly killed me when I saw his face as I told him I was leaving. Three thousand miles. I didn't know if it was far enough away to get over him, but I knew it was hurting him. His best friend was abandoning him.

"I'm sorry, Drake," I whispered.

He didn't say a word as he turned and walked away. As the door shut quietly behind him, I crumbled to the floor, shattered all over again.

Chapter 9
Drake

Over the last three weeks, I had heard them all. Excuse after excuse, and they all ended with the same phrase: "…and then I hit rock bottom and ended up here." *Here* was the best rehab in the country. The one place I hoped to find solace after the mess I had made of my life because I had hit rock bottom, and now I was free falling toward Hell.

In the three weeks, I had been here, I hadn't had one drink. I was shaky, fingers trembling just at the thought of a bottle of any kind of alcohol. Depression was a painful thing. It made your entire body ache for no good reason. My chest constantly felt like there was someone standing on it. Sometimes at night I couldn't sleep from the sheer pain of not having my angel close. There was nothing—not one damned thing—that I could do about it.

The staff, from the nurses to the psychiatrists, all said I was doing well. I thought they were full of shit. I was a mess. Without the alcohol I was haunted day and night, not only by nightmares of the day I had beaten my stepdad half to death, but now I had one more torment to add to all the others.

Lana's face as she told me she loved me, but that I had ruined everything.

Emmie had called me the night before and asked if I was coming home next week, when my thirty days was up. I wanted to see her so badly. I had never spent this long away from her, but I knew that if I really wanted to get through this I needed to stay another thirty days…

Today, I was having a one-on-one session with my psychiatrist. It was the first time I had ever sought the guy out instead of him having to seek me out. He said that step alone was progress, but I thought he was delusional. I spent ten minutes just staring out his window at the lake off in the distance before I even started talking about what was on my mind, but he give me time and space.

Finally, I blew out a long breath and raked a hand through my hair in frustration. "I was sixteen when I opened the first bottle. The first swallow was like swallowing a mouthful of fire, but the burn was a good one. It took my mind off of what I wanted to forget. The second swallow was a little easier to get down, and by the third I was out of it."

The doctor, a skinny man with long gray hair pulled back into a ponytail and eyes that looked like he had seen it all in his profession, simply nodded. "How did you feel later, after the effects wore off?"

"Worst headache of my life," I assured him. "My mom..." I swallowed hard. I rarely talked about my mother. It was just too painful to think about her. "My mom thought I had the flu and stayed home from work to take care of me."

"Do you want to talk about your mom, Drake?" Dr. Kent asked, having seen me flinch at the mention of my mother.

I sighed and locked my fingers together behind my head. "Not really," I muttered.

Kent was quiet for a long moment, as if he were giving me time to rethink my answer. When he finally did speak, he surprised me. "Your brother has come to visit you a few times, but he never stays long. Why is that?"

Pain sliced through my chest thinking about Shane and his last visit, just the day before. Lana was gone. She was in New York now, three thousand miles away. I hadn't gotten to tell her goodbye or that I loved her. She was just gone, off starting a new life that I had no place in.

"He just wants to see how I am," I told the doctor, "but he knows that I will want to leave with him if he stays too long." Yesterday had been one of those days when I had nearly begged my little brother to get me the hell out of this place. I wanted to get on a plane and follow Lana across the country!

The only thing stopping me was the knowledge that I wasn't in the right frame of mind to be with Lana just now. First, I had to become a man that was deserving of my angel. The man I had been three weeks ago, when I had walked through the front doors of this place that was so private it didn't even have a name, didn't deserve Lana. I was working toward being one that did.

"Maybe we should sit down and have a group session. Me, you, and your brother. Perhaps, the only way to sort out your past is to face it head on. Do you think he would be open to that?"

I glared at the doctor. "I don't want to put Shane through that."

The doctor let it go, and I spent the rest of the session just staring out the window again...

When I walked into Kent's office the next morning, after a nurse had informed me that I was to have a session with the doctor again, I wasn't pleased to find my brother sitting on the long sofa in front of the doctor's usual chair.

"What the fuck?" I exploded and faced the doctor, who was sitting calmly behind his desk. "I told you I didn't want to do this!"

"Dray, I want to be here," Shane said, and I turned around to look at him. He looked pale, and I could see that his hands were fisted at his sides, but there was determination in his blue-gray eyes.

"I don't want to put you through this," I told my little brother, the urge to protect him still eating at me. "You don't have to..."

Shane was already shaking his head. "I think it will be good for both of us, bro. Just give it a chance."

I frowned at him for a long moment. It went against everything that was inside of me, but I finally sat down beside him. The doctor stood and moved to his chair across from us, his iPad in hand. "I agree with you, Shane. I think this will be a good thing for you both."

"Emmie thinks so too, or I wouldn't be here," Shane assured the man who grinned at the mention of Em.

"Well, I'm sure if she agrees then we can't go wrong." He typed something into the iPad and then put it on the table between us. "Let's start off simply by talking about your mother."

Even as my whole body tensed, I could sense Shane's doing the same. "Our mom was one of the best women I have ever known," Shane began after a static filled minute. "I always like to remember her as the saving grace to everything else that was bad in the world."

It hurt to hear Shane talking about the woman that had been everything to us both. She had been a great mom, working hard to support my brother and me to make sure that we never wanted for anything. Our dad had been a decent enough guy, when he was around, but once he had gotten married again, and that marriage had produced a few more kids, we might as well not have existed for all the attention he showed us.

"How did your mother die?" Kent asked after Shane had told him all about the wonderful woman that had given us both life.

I watched Shane's throat work a few times before he whispered out the answer. "She killed herself... It was all my fault."

I jumped to my feet, already fighting tears but also angry. "What?" I exploded. "How can you say that? It wasn't your fault, Shane. It was mine."

My brother scrubbed a hand over his damp eyes and got to his feet to face me. "No. You didn't do anything wrong. You saved Emmie. You avenged me and yourself. I'm the one who told Mom what Rusty did. I'm the one who stood by and did nothing while she grabbed the cop's gun and killed him. I didn't stop her when she turned the gun on herself!"

The tears poured down both our faces now, but I didn't care. It was tearing me apart inside to hear those words coming from Shane. That he had blamed himself all these years was just wrong on so many levels. "No one knew she was going to do that, Shane. She...She just..." My voice broke when Shane started sobbing. "No, Shane. Please." I pulled him into my arms, holding onto the man that was still the boy trapped in the past. "I'm sorry, little brother. It was all my fault. If I had just told someone, then none of it would ever have happened."

"You were just trying to protect me, Dray," Shane managed through his sobs, "like you always do, and I love you for that." He pulled back a little to meet my gaze. "You have to stop blaming yourself, brother. Let it all go, man. Let it go."

Chapter 10
July
Lana

My cellphone was buzzing from my back pocket with Jesse's text tone that I had assigned months ago. It was an annoying sound that I had thought was appropriate because he only ever texted me with annoying news. Still, I loved him and I knew that he loved me, so I fished the cell from my hip pocket and opened the text.

Picking you up @ 6. Be ready.

I frowned. What was he doing in New York? I knew for a fact that Demon's Wings didn't have a concert. The band only did small tours, and they didn't have an East Coast tour scheduled until next spring. My brother-in-law being in New York out of the blue startled me and made me wonder if everything was okay back home.

Is everything ok? I rushed to ask.

Need to see you. Be ready.

"Fuck," I muttered, stepping into my apartment building. Normally, I would have greeted the doorman, but I was just too preoccupied to even notice him. The ride up to the twelfth floor felt like it took forever, and by the time I stepped through the door of the three bedroom corner apartment, I was biting my nails to the quick.

I tossed my shoulder bag on the sofa and flopped down, glaring at the TV that was already on some sports show. Looked like Linc was already home from the gym. "Are you in the kitchen?" I called out.

"Yeah. You want something?" my deep voiced roommate called back.

"Got anything harder than beer? I need a drink." He knew that I was kidding. I had only gotten drunk once since moving to New York. That night had been bad, and I didn't want to relive it.

"How about a pint of Ben & Jerry's and some hot fudge?" He appeared at the end of the couch with the ice cream in one hand and the hot fudge in the other. One look at my face and the hulky man dropped down beside me. "What's up?"

"My brother-in-law is picking me up at six."

"Jesse Thornton, right?" I nodded. "So what's the problem?"

"It's a surprise visit. I don't know why he's here, and all he said when I asked was that he needed to see me." I pushed my hair away from my face. "He never does things like this, and I'm worried something is wrong."

Linc cracked his neck, making me grimace. It was what he always did when he was thinking. After spending the last seven months under the same roof with him, and my two other roommates, I knew all his little quirks. "I guess you will just have to wait and see," he finally said.

I glared at him. "Thanks for those words of wisdom, babe." I rolled my eyes at him and took the ice cream.

He winked as he got to his feet. "Anytime, sweets. Anytime."

I threw the lid at his retreating back. It bounced off his hard ass and landed on the end of the couch. "Where are Dallas and Harper? I figured they would be back by now."

"Still shopping."

I hoped they would be back before Jesse got here. It was already after four, and I needed my two best friends here to diffuse the whole "Linc is living in the apartment" situation. It wasn't like he didn't know that I had a male roommate. I had told Layla and Jesse all about him. Fitness model, check. Good friend, check. Gay, double check.

91

Linc was all of those things. But looking at him, talking to him, you would never guess that he was one of the gayest men on the planet. He was sexy as sin, and I will honestly admit that when the dude walked around in little to nothing—okay, sometimes nothing at all!—I wasn't shy about looking. Neither were Harper and Dallas.

Still, it was going to be hard to convince Jesse that big, hulking, sin on two legs Linc Spencer was the guy I had told him all about. When I had first met Linc, I hadn't believed that he was gay either. It had taken him bringing some random guy home from a club one night to make me believe. And only then when they had started making some very X-rated sounds from the bedroom across from the one I shared with Harper.

Yeah, Jesse was going to hit the roof when he showed up to pick me up.

At five, my roommates still weren't home, and I rushed to get ready. By ten to six, I was ready and waiting, impatient to get this over with. I was almost tempted to ask Linc to hide when Jesse got here but didn't want to hurt my friend's feelings. He was a Demon's Wings fan and would want to meet Jesse.

The door opening startled me, and I looked up to find both Harper and Dallas entering the apartment. Each had their arms loaded with bags, and I figured Dallas was being rebellious again and maxing out her mother's credit cards. Her hair was pulled back from her face, exposing the dimple in her right cheek. She had been one of Europe's highest paid models from the age of fifteen until last year when she had turned twenty-one.

That was when her contract had come up for renewal with her agent and she had refused to sign on again. Modeling had never been her thing. In fact, she hated every second of it. Her mother had been the one to force Dallas into it and signed the original contract, making her unable to get out of it until it ran out. When Dallas had refused to continue, her mother had gone ballistic.

Since then, she had made sure that her mother wouldn't want her to do the model thing. She had tattooed and pierced her body until her mother nearly had a stroke from just looking at her. I applauded Dallas' rebellion. It was her body, after all.

Of course I had lent my support and went to get a tattoo with her on Valentines' Day. My first ink had left me with an addiction for it. I was already thinking of what I wanted next, and this time I was going to go all out with a big piece of ink on my back. Compared to Dallas, Harper looked like a librarian in her cashmere skirt and cardigan. Her caramel colored hair was pulled back in a French braid and her glasses hid those lavender eyes of hers. I had met Harper my first day of NYU, and we had become friends fast. When my roommate had gone all psychotic bitch on me the second week of spring term, and I had needed a place to stay, she offered me the twin bed in her room.

"Hey, you should see the car downstairs," Harper said as she dropped down beside me on the couch. "Stretch limo in front of this building? That just seems too funny."

I grimaced. "That's probably Jesse."

Harper's eyes grew huge behind her dark frames. "What's he doing here? Did you know he was coming?"

I shook my head. "Not until about two hours ago." I stood and smoothed a hand over my sundress, a gift from Dallas the last time her mother had pissed her off and she had gone Fifth Avenue crazy on her mom's cards.

Just as I slipped on my wedges, the phone rang. Dallas picked it up because she was the closest to it. "Yes?" she asked, her southern accent never failing to make me smile. "Oh. Okay. He can come up." She replaced the phone and grinned at me. "Rock star in the building!"

Linc came out of his room down the hall. His hair was damp and all he was wearing was a pair of basketball shorts and a smile. My mind went blank for a moment as I drooled over the sight of all those hard angled abs and tight pecks. And then I remembered that Jesse was on his way up in the elevator and Linc was running around half naked.

"Put a shirt on!" I said, pushing him back down the hall to his room. "And some pants. Your free balling and I don't want my brother-in-law getting hysterical about you walking around with your junk hanging free!"

Linc laughed. "Oh my God, Lana! Relax. I can handle your in-law."

I pushed him hard. "Go, Linc. Please." The doorbell rang and I jumped. "Please," I cried. He didn't know Jesse like I did. I didn't want my friend with a broken nose or something bleeding.

Harper was already standing by the door. "Wait!" I called to her, making sure the door to Linc's room was closed behind him before letting her answering the door. "Okay, go ahead," I said, smoothing my dress down once again.

Harper giggled and pulled the door open. I wasn't ready, but then I doubted I ever would be.

When I saw Jesse standing in the door way my heart hurt. I hadn't seen him since he and Layla had flown out to New York with me in January. He looked good, especially in his suit. Despite the anxiety I felt over his reaction to Linc, I found myself running across the living room and throwing my arms around Jesse.

Strong arms tightened around me as he lifted me off the ground in a bear hug. He laughed and swung me around once before setting me on my feet. "It's good to see you, Lana."

I had to blink to keep the tears from falling. "I don't know why you're here, but I'm so happy to see you."

His eyes darkened, changing colors rapidly. "We can talk later." His raised his eyes to look at Harper and then Dallas.

This was the first time he had seen my roommates and best friends. "Hello, ladies," he greeted with an easy smile.

"Oh shit." Dallas fanned herself with her hand. "You are hotter in person than I expected."

I rolled my eyes at her. "Jess, this is Dallas Bradshaw and that's Harper Jones." I introduced them. "Guys, you know who he is, so whatever."

Harper giggled and offered Jesse her hand. "Nice to finally meet you, Jesse."

"You too, Harper." He winked at Dallas who was still sitting on the couch. "And you're the trash mouth I keep hearing in the background when Layla calls."

Dallas shrugged. "I do what I can."

Jesse glanced around. "And the other roommate? Linc, right?"

I mentally groaned and prayed that Linc wouldn't come out. Of course he picked that moment to open his bedroom door. I closed my eyes, waiting for the explosion that was sure to erupt. "Hey, man. I'm Linc."

Cautiously, I peeked open one eye, glancing at Jesse. His eyes narrowed at the other man, but he wasn't sprouting curses or swinging fists. I took it as a good sign but didn't want to push my luck, so I pulled Jesse toward the door. "I assume you are taking me to dinner. I'm starving, let's go."

He was quiet all the way down in the elevator, his big hands thrust into the pockets of his suit pants. There was a driver standing by the door to the limo, and I gave him a small smile as he opened it for me. When we were settled inside, the limo pulled out into traffic. "Okay, let's hear it."

"That guy is gay?" he exploded. "No way. He can't be..."

I grinned. "And you would know...how?"

"Don't get cute with me, Lana. Your sister is going to shit a brick!"

I cocked a brow at him. "Are you sure you're worried about Layla's reaction? Or someone else's?"

95

"Lana..." He rubbed a hand over his smooth head, telling me that he was frustrated. "Let's wait and talk when we get to the restaurant. Please?"

"Only if you tell me this doesn't have something to do with Layla or Lucy? Are they okay?"

"Both are fine. And Layla is here with me. She's going to join us later."

Excitement shot through me. I talked to my sister every day, but a phone call didn't make up for getting to see Layla. My excitement was short lived because I knew that if this wasn't about either of my sisters, then that only left one other reason for Jesse to be here like this. I turned my head away so he couldn't see my expression and gazed out the side window as the limo drove through Wednesday evening traffic in New York City.

The restaurant the limo stopped in front of was so popular there was a six month waiting list for reservations. I had only heard about it, and I really hadn't had any real urge to try the place out. Expensive food only gave me indigestion, especially when I was presented with the bill.

I figured we would have to wait for a table, but I guess Emmie had worked her magic and had gotten Jesse a quiet table in the back. People actually stopped eating as we passed, and I couldn't help but feel self-conscious. When we reached our table, I breathed a sigh of relief.

"Really? You had to bring me here?"

Jesse grinned. "Yes. I had to bring you here."

"Why? Couldn't you have just taken me to McDonald's and bought me a cheeseburger?" That was more me. This place? Not so much!

The waiter brought wine, which I didn't want. Jesse ignored his glass in favor of his water. I didn't bother to glance at the menu. It was probably in French or some other language anyway. Instead, I glared at the man seated across me. "I'm getting impatient, Jesse."

96

He blew out a long sigh. "I know. I'm trying to work up to it." I rolled my eyes and he laughed. "We all miss you, you know. It's the little things that make me think about you."

"I miss you too, Jess."

Jesse tossed his menu aside and reached for my hands. "There's something I want to talk to you about. I need you to really listen, okay?"

"Okay."

"There is a new show that's starting in September. It's called America's Rocker." He rolled his eyes when I laughed. Yeah, okay. "Axton Cage was asked to sit on the panel of judges, but one of the other two judges backed out, and Ax said that he wanted someone from Demon's Wings or he was backing out too. The network agreed."

I frowned. "So are you going to be in New York more?" I smiled. "That's great, Jesse!" I would get to see him and my sisters often.

He was shaking his head. "Nik and I both turned it down, and Emmie was about to tell the network to get lost when Drake agreed to do it."

I sat up straighter in my chair. "What?"

"Everything is taking place here in New York. Everything. The tryouts, the show, the finale. Drake will be here next week. Emmie has already found him an apartment. Shane is coming out here with him."

I ran a trembling hand through my hair. I hadn't spoken to Drake since before I had moved to New York. Somehow, I had succeeded in avoiding him until I left. It had killed something inside of me when I left, unable to tell him goodbye, but as the weeks went by and I settled into my new life, things had gotten better. My heart was still shattered, but at least I had swept up the pieces.

Through Jesse and Layla, and even Shane, I had heard that Drake had checked himself into rehab and actually finished it this time. It had been big news in the rock world for about a week. Drake Stevenson sober. It had been a miracle, everyone said. People wondered what had brought on the sudden need to clean up his act.

I talked to Shane regularly, and he always took the chance to tell me that his brother was doing well. Always telling me how many days Drake had been sober, like it was a new mile stone, and really it was. I was proud of him, but that didn't stop my heart from aching.

It didn't stop me from wanting him to hold me every night.

But I had given up hope of that ever happening a long time ago.

Chapter 11

Lana

When I had first gotten to New York, part of me—a really big part—had hoped that it would force Drake to realize that he was in love with me. I had lain in bed for two weeks straight, mentally willing him to come after me. Every day, I would search the crowd looking for him. Any guy with overly long, dark hair would make me stop, and I would hold my breath, only to be disappointed when I would realize that it wasn't Drake.

When I had moved into the apartment with Harper, I stopped crying myself to sleep. I learned to live with the pain, and without realizing it, the pain slowly got easier to deal with. That didn't mean I didn't think about him. No, he was on my mind every five minutes. The littlest things would remind me of him.

Some might think that keeping tabs on Drake through his brother was just feeding my pain, but it helped. Knowing that he was okay gave me some peace, and getting to talk to Shane gave me the smallest of connection to Drake, which I hung onto by my fingernails.

It had also made Shane and me closer. He was a big part of my day to day, even if I hadn't seen him in seven months. If I went a day without talking to him, it made me sad. If I missed one of his calls, he blew up my phone with texts until I called him back. Maybe he was keeping tabs on me for his brother, but I didn't care.

Now, as I stared at my phone after having just gotten home from dinner with Jesse and my sister, I couldn't help but wonder what the younger Stevenson brother was up too. It was after eleven here, so that meant it was still early in California, just after eight. More than likely he hadn't gone out yet.

Sighing, I pulled up his name on my phone and hit send. It rang three times before he answered. "You didn't tell me," I said when I heard his voice on the other end.

"Jesse wanted to tell you first," he assured me, knowing exactly what I was talking about without having to ask. "So... What do you think? We can hang out when I get into town."

"Why would he do this, Shane? He hates attention like this, and now he's going to put himself front and center on a freaking reality television show." I closed my eyes, a headache making my eyes throb.

Shane paused, as if thinking about what to say before he spoke. "He has his reasons, Lana. Maybe one day he will tell you about them. Until then, let's talk about you and me and the best burger in the world. I know this great burger joint, and I want to take you there."

Rolling my eyes, I lay back on the couch. Might as well get comfortable. "When do you get in?"

"Tuesday. Drake has to be there for tryouts on Friday, and he wants to be settled in by then. So, let's go out Thursday. I'll pick you up...unless you want to come over to our apartment?"

"Um, no. That's okay." I wasn't sure I was ready to see Drake face to face yet. "Thursday is fine. I'll stay home and wait with bated breath for your arrival, stud."

He chuckled. "Great. And then Friday you can show me the best jogging trail to take through Central Park."

"I don't run through the park. I go to the gym and use the treadmills."

"No way! I'm ashamed of you, Lana! Okay, then we will find them together. After the burgers we are going to need the exercise...Ah, crap!"

"What?" I demanded, startled when I heard someone else's voice in the background. Was that a girl? "Shane, really? Next time I call and you're with some skank, do me a favor and don't answer!"

"I'm not with some skank, Lana!" Shane assured me. "I'm meeting Emmie and Nik for dinner. That was the waitress."

"Sure it was." I laughed. "Liar. I'll let you go so you can get to your...dinner."

"You are such a bitch sometimes," he muttered.

"Yeah, I know. See you Thursday."

"Can't wait. Love ya, sweetheart."

"Love you too, Shane." With a quivering chin, I hit the end button and tossed my phone aside.

--

It felt like Thursday took forever to come around. My roommates avoided me at times because I was equal parts anxious and excited and that made for horrible mood swings. Linc kept giving me the evil eye, not sure if my behavior was from PMS or if I was just being my sometimes bitchy self.

I had one class Thursday morning. Trying to cram three months of Biology material into five weeks over the summer break was not fun, but I was glad for the challenge. Still, as soon as my professor excused us, I pulled out my cell to see if I had missed any texts from Shane.

Pick you up @ 1. Can't wait for dinner 2 c u.

A glance at the clock on my phone told me that I wasn't going to make it to my apartment in time unless I grabbed a cab. Muttering a curse, I flagged one down and tossed the driver an incentive to get me home as quick as he could. New York cab drivers in a hurry made for a terrifying ride. I just covered my eyes and waited for the car to finally come to a stop.

Paying my fare, I grabbed my shoulder bag that held all my essentials and turned for the apartment. The tall man standing by the door made me stop. He was just standing there watching me. I couldn't see those blue-gray eyes of his behind the sunglasses, and his Boston Red Sox cap was on backwards, hiding that shaggy dark hair from me. He hadn't changed in the seven months since I had last seen him.

With a delighted squeal, I jumped the few feet separating us and threw my legs around his waist. "It's so good to see you," I said, hugging him tight.

He laughed, swinging me around and around. It didn't seem to matter to him that we were on a busy sidewalk, or that people had to stop and walk around us. Shane was the kind of man that didn't care about public displays of any kind.

"I was going crazy back in the apartment. All I could think about was that I was going to get to see my favorite girl in the world and I couldn't wait." He sat me on my feet, scanning me from head to toe behind those shades of his.

"Wow!" He shook his head. "More beautiful than I remember." His fingers touched my hair, which was longer now than it had been the last time he had seen me. "Okay, sis. Let's get going before I start having thoughts that could get me killed."

I slapped his arm, knowing that he was completely kidding. "Do you want to come up?" I motioned to my shoulder bag. "I want to get rid of this thing before we go traipsing around the city."

He followed me into the building, and I stopped at the doorman's desk. After making sure that Shane was on my list of approved guests, we took the elevator up to my floor. I knew that everyone was home before I had even unlocked the door. I could hear Linc and Dallas arguing, something that didn't even faze me these day.

I glanced at Shane. "Keep an open mind, okay?" I told him, trying to prepare him for Linc. I had learned, after my gaffe of not believing Linc was gay, that his type was the pretty boy type. And you didn't get prettier than Shane. He and his brother were borderline beautiful, in a masculine way, and Linc was going to be on red alert.

"Sure." He nodded.

Opening the door, I found my roommates spread out around the living room watching the Style Network. No wonder Dallas and Linc were arguing. Dallas knew most of the models on there—had actually been one of them—and knew all their dirty secrets. Linc, who was friends with several of those models, didn't want to believe Dallas.

Harper, looking bored with the whole thing—the conversation and the television show—skimmed through a copy of *The New Yorker*. Three pair of eyes turned their full attention on me as I pulled Shane into the apartment. I saw Linc's blue eyes light up, and I narrowed my own at him.

"Hey, look who I found!"

Dallas gave Shane a once over then another one just for good measure. I glanced at Shane who had his eyes narrowed on Linc, not even noticing the interest in the ex-top model's eyes. "You're Linc?" he demanded.

"Yep. That's me." Linc grinned, liking the attention.

"Well, there's something we can talk about later," Shane muttered to me. "Drake is going to shit a brick."

I stiffened. "This is none of Drake's business."

"Oh, I think it is." He pushed his sun glasses on top of his head. "But whatever, sis, we can talk about it later."

I gave him a hard glare and pushed him toward the couch. "Guys, this is Shane. Shane, these are my roommates. Linc, of course. Dallas, who seems to be eye-fucking you..." I shot her a wink, knowing that I would get bitched at later "...and this is my bestie, Harper."

Harper waved but went back to reading. She wasn't fazed in the least by Shane's complete hotness. My friend had a big self-esteem problem. She had no idea that she was drop dead gorgeous and never suspected when guys were interested. I shot Shane a warning look and went to change clothes.

Ten minutes later, I came out of the bedroom I shared with Harper to find everyone laughing in the living room. I stopped, taking them all in before they could notice me. Shane had the ability to put anyone at ease. It surprised me that he had picked the part of the couch closest to Harper, when Dallas had been giving him the green light with her eyes from the moment she had seen him.

He said something that I didn't hear, and Harper snorted with laughter. It was then that I saw it, the way his eyes danced when he looked at her. Shane had been presented with a challenge when Harper had showed disinterest. He was used to every woman he came across giving in, and now he had found one that didn't really give a fuck about falling into his bed.

Muttering a curse under my breath, I made a mental note to kick Shane Stevenson's ass while I was out with him today.

--

The best burger in the world was in my stomach, and I felt like I had gained fifteen pounds. I was stuffed to the point of pain, and it was all Shane's fault.

As we left the little Mom and Pop place, I groaned, trying to figure out how to make this full feeling go away. The rock star beside me probably wasn't enduring the same pain as me. He had finished his burger, and half of my own, as well as two orders of fries and some onion rings. With all the junk he had put away during our meal, which had included Shane ordering a huge hot fudge ice cream dessert that I hadn't been able to even look at because I was so full, I couldn't help but wonder if he ate like that normally. Emmie probably attempted to keep the saturated fat to a minimum, but now that he was three thousand miles away from her, he was taking advantage. I would have to keep an eye on that and let Emmie know if he kept it up. I took an evil delight in possibly tattling on him.

"You look miserable." Shane laughed as he pulled me close. He turned right and I didn't even question him as we started walking. I needed the exercise after all.

"I am, but it was worth it. That was the best burger I have ever had. Thanks. I'll have to let Linc know about that place."

"About Linc..." Shane grimaced. "Is he really gay, Lana? I mean, really?"

I couldn't help but snicker. "I didn't believe it at first either, but yes, he is very gay. I guess you would say he's butch?" I shrugged. "I'm not sure what the correct term for him is." My grin was wicked. "If it helps, you're his type. Linc loves a man with a pretty face."

His big hand swatted against my ass, making me squeal. "You mean little bitch!"

My laugh was soul deep. "Just thought you would want to know."

"Gee, thanks, but I'm going to have to say it's a definite no this time around." We stopped to wait for the light to turn so we could cross the street. "Although, if you could help me out with your friend Harper..."

I pushed him away. "No way! Stay away from Harper. She's not your type."

"Sis, I don't have a type," he said with a smirk.

"That's the problem. Harper isn't the kind of girl to come running when you cock your sexy finger." The light turned and we started across the street. "She's a good girl. Not one of those groupie skanks that you and your brother are used to. Especially what you are used to."

"That's harsh, sis." He gripped his heart, a pout on his lips. "You wound me."

"Oh, please. You have loved maybe one girl in your whole life, and she's going to marry your best friend."

"Not true." He wrapped his arm around my waist again, holding me protectively to his side as we walked with and against the evening crowd. "I actually love five girls. Emmie, Mia, Lucy, Layla, and you."

Chapter 12
Drake

I was supposed to be at the network's studio by eight. I got there on time with the help of the car and driver that the network had sent, but the line outside the studio made me ten minutes late because it was wrapped all the way around the building and two blocks past it. Fans, tryout hopefuls, and their friends and family that had come to support said hopefuls made it slow going for a while as the driver attempted to get through the masses without running anyone over.

By the time I got inside, the producers were already bitching, but I was used to that shit from Emmie after so many years, so I tuned it out and fell into my designated chair next to Axton. My friend was sucking down scalding coffee like it was nothing while he eye-fucked the producer's assistant. Apparently he was over the big and final—thank fuck—breakup from Gabriella Moreitti.

The chair on Axton's left was still vacant, and I wondered who the top secret third judge was for this stupid reality show. Not even Axton knew who the network had gotten, and he had been signed on to do this thing since February.

Someone set a huge mug of coffee down in front of me, and I nodded my head in thanks without giving the girl so much as a glance. I had already downed an entire pot of coffee since six o'clock that morning. Which was about the time I had heard Shane leave for his run...

Gritting my teeth, I pushed thoughts of my little brother, and who he could possibly be with right now, out of my mind as the producer finally got his shit together and started giving orders to his other staff members to get the tryout hopefuls organized outside.

"How you liking New York?" Axton asked as he bit into some kind of pastry.

I shrugged. "It's New York."

Axton raised a brow, making his eyebrow ring glint in the overhead lighting. "You haven't even left the apartment yet, have you? Dude, you are really sad since you quit drinking."

I snorted. "Thanks, man. I love you too."

"I didn't say I didn't love ya, Dray. Just that you are really sad. Grab that brother of yours and let's do something we shouldn't tonight."

I shook my head. "Nah, I'm good." There was only one thing I wanted to do, and I wasn't sure how I was going to accomplish it. I knew that hanging out with Axton and getting into something I shouldn't would only make everything that much worse.

The door I had entered a little while ago opened, and everyone including myself turned to see who the late arrival was. I nearly fell out of my seat when I recognized Cole Steel of Steel Entrapment walking in like he owned the place. Knowing that old rocker, he probably did, or at least a share in it. He and his band had retired a decade or so ago, but they had remained in the business through other means. Cole owned half of a record label and backed several producing studios.

No wonder the network had kept their lips so tightly closed about Cole being the third judge. It was going to send ratings through the roof with the surprise coming out just weeks before the show went on the air. Axton shook his head. "Motherfucker!"

"Morning boys," the fifty-something rocker greeted in his gravelly voice. Years of smoking had altered his voice. Some thought he had had throat cancer a few years ago, but it was only a nodule on his vocal cord that had been removed. Still, he probably would never be able to sing again, at least not like he once had.

107

I shook Cole's hand. "Goddamn, man, I didn't think I would see you here," I told him.

"The money was just too sweet to turn down." Cole shrugged as he took his seat on the other side of Axton.

With all of us now accounted for, the producers gave us a rundown of what was on the books for today. An itinerary was provided, and I scanned it before pushing it away. This was going to be boring as hell!

Two hours later, I was almost falling asleep in my chair as we went through one tryout hopeful after another. No one had stood out. No one had really caught my attention. So far, everyone had been so nervous that they hadn't lasted more than a minute before they were being excused from the room. Some of these people had spent thousands of dollars on airfare, hotel rooms, and countless other things just to come here and bomb within minutes of standing before three judges.

The producer called for a break, and I reached for my phone. It had vibrated three different times in the last ten minutes. Sliding my finger across the screen, I saw messages from Emmie and Shane waiting for me. I took care of Emmie first because that was more important. She was going to freak when I told her who the third judge was.

Finally, I pulled up the message from Shane and nearly dropped my phone when I saw the attached photo he had sent me. I didn't know whether to hunt my little brother down and murder him or thank him as I gazed down at Lana's smiling face staring back at me. Her long midnight black hair was pulled into a ponytail and she was wearing some kind of tight running suit that made her whiskey eyes stand out.

I stared down at the picture until the producers started letting more tryout hopefuls in before saving it to my phone. I felt more awake now, and I was actually paying more attention as the day went on.

--

I was at the network's studio until almost ten that night. The line outside was still growing by that time. I was beat and my head was killing me. Everyone who was in line was told that tryouts would begin again at eight the next morning, and I wasn't surprised that the majority of them decided to camp out.

My driver picked me up and drove me back to my apartment. Shane had texted me throughout the day, and with each passing message I looked forward to hearing from my brother. He had spent the day with Lana, and it almost felt as if I had too the way my brother had kept sending me pictures of her.

When the car pulled to a stop in front of my building, I got out and nodded to the night doorman as I headed for the elevators. "Good evening, Mr. Stevenson. Your brother asked me to tell you he was taking the young lady home since you had taken so long."

I stopped. "The young lady?"

The middle aged man nodded. "Yes. Miss Daniels I believe is her name. The other Mr. Stevenson made sure that she was put on your list of guests to let up without having to ask your permission."

I muttered a curse, beyond disappointed that Lana had been inside my apartment and I hadn't gotten to see her. She had actually been here! My chest ached and I pulled my cell out as I stepped onto the elevator. It rang once before Shane's distracted voice greeted me.

"What?" he asked, an amused note in his tone.

"She was here?"

"Yup. I'm leaving her place now. I'll see you in a few."

"Dammit!" I raked a hand through my hair. "I want to see her!"

Shane sighed. "Yeah, I know. I did my best, bro. But you were taking for-freaking-ever."

"What about tomorrow? Are you going to see her tomorrow?"

"No, man. She has plans. I'll keep trying though. Okay?"

I blew out a long sigh. What more could I ask? I knew it was going to be an uphill battle to get Lana back in my life. I had fucked up, lost the best thing that had ever happened to me. But I had worked hard to get to a place so I could be worthy of her...

Rehab had been a nightmare. The past—the guilt—had been hard to let go of. But Emmie, Shane, and the rest of my band brothers had helped me through it. They had been my support system through those long miserable two months, and then afterward when I had gotten home. Shane went with me to AA meetings, and Emmie was always offering me encouragement.

I had been sober for seven months and sixteen days.

Was it enough to win back the woman I loved?

"Yeah. Okay." The elevator came to a slow stop on my floor and I stepped out. "Thanks, Shane...I really appreciate it, brother."

Chapter 13
Drake

Tryouts had been held for two solid weeks now, which meant that I was getting up at the ass-crack of dawn and getting home late as fuck!

So far we had narrowed down thousands of hopefuls to about a hundred, most of them guys. The few females that had made it through had been exceptionally good and even made me snap out of my funk to take notice. The three of us all had to agree before a hopeful got to go on to the next round, which didn't take place until September. I only gave my *yes* if they really made me take notice of them. If they didn't have what it took to make me look twice at them, then they weren't worth my time.

Axton was a little easier to appease, but it was Cole who was the real hard ass. He had been in the business for more than half his life, and he knew what to really look for in a rock star. More than once he had made grown men burst into tears because he had told them exactly what he thought of them and their *talent*.

To say I was tired of spending every free moment at the studio was the understatement of the decade. I hated every second of it, regretted ever agreeing to do this stupid thing in the first place. The only reason I had done so was because it had given me the chance to come to New York. I had a reason to be closer to Lana and I had jumped in feet first. Of course I hadn't known that I wouldn't have five fucking minutes to breathe, let alone plan how I was going to win my angel back.

Today, the producers were letting some fans in as a kind of audience. I had ignored each set of them because they changed every two hours or so. All I wanted was to get through this day and get home at a decent hour for once. I had even brought Shane along today in hopes of making the producers annoyed enough to call an end to the auditions early.

At the moment, the producer's assistants were showing in another group of fans. I didn't bother to look over at them as I sketched a pair of angel wings on the edge of my itinerary. Axton was surfing the web on his phone, glancing up with a grin every now and then when one of the female fans called out that she loved him.

"Holy Fuck!" he muttered next to me. "How do I get that in my bed?"

Curious, I followed his gaze. There was a blonde sitting in the back. She was gorgeous; I'd give her that. Tall, sitting higher than any of the other females and even some of the guys, she wasn't really paying attention to what was going on around her. Instead, she was playing with something on her phone. There was an empty seat beside her, but I didn't really pay attention to it.

"She's hot," I agreed.

"Dude, seriously. She's beyond hot. Me want. Me want bad."

I laughed for the first time that day, maybe even the first time in weeks. "Then tell the producer prick you want a break and go get her number."

"Hey!" Axton waved his hand until the blonde raised her head. "Hey, you! What's your name?"

I snorted, my stomach hurting from holding in my laughter. "Smooth," I muttered.

The girl frowned. "Me?" she called back.

"Yes, of course you!" Axton shouted. "What's your name, hotness?"

"None of your fucking business! If you can't come talk to me like a decent human being would, then you don't need to know." She shot him the finger and turned her attention back to her phone.

112

I was still laughing when the next hopeful stepped inside. Poor kid was nervous as hell and didn't last more than two minutes before Cole was thanking him for his time. I went back to my sketch...

A door shutting just behind the fans caught my attention and I glanced up, expecting to see one of them going in search of a bathroom. The sight that greeted me made me feel as if I had been punched in the gut, the oxygen leaving my lungs so fast.

She was here! Oh fuck, she was beautiful!

Lana stood at the back of the group. Her hair, longer than I remembered it, was flowing freely down her slender back. She was wearing jean shorts and a Demon's Wings shirt that I had given her when we had first met. As I watched, she dropped down into the chair next to the blonde. The other girl whispered something to her, shooting Axton evil glances.

"Hotness' friend looks familiar," Axton commented.

"Keep your fucking eyes to yourself," I bit out, keeping my eyes locked on Lana. "If you look at her the wrong way I will hit you so hard you will puke out your balls."

Axton snorted, not intimidated by my threat in the least. "Chill out, man...Oh, shit. That's Lana!"

He said it loud enough that her head snapped around. Whiskey colored eyes locked with mine, and I was defenseless to look away. After a long moment, her lips tilted ever so slightly and she gave me a small smile. Not one of my hard to perfect on paper Angel smiles, but I would take what I could get. She raised a hand, giving a tiny wave.

"If you two are done eye-fucking the ho-club," Cole commented from the end of the table, "I think the next loser is about to come in."

Lana

I must have had a moment of insanity.

113

When Shane had texted me that morning saying the studio was allowing fans to watch the auditions for the show, I should have just turned over and gone back to sleep. But what had I done? I had jumped into the shower and was ready in less than half an hour!

Somehow, I had conned Dallas into going with me. My first choice would have been Harper, but she had to work this morning. Freelance photographers never knew when they were going to get a call, and right now Harper was pretty popular with some of the more respectable magazines. Still, I was happy that Dallas had taken the time from pissing her mother off to come with me.

We waited in a long line with other fans to get in. They were taking everyone back in groups of twenty-five to thirty at a time for two hour time intervals. Dallas and I had been pretty far back in the line, but I had texted Shane and he had sent someone to take us with the next group.

I was nervous. My hands were sweaty and my heart was racing. I wasn't sure if I was ready to see Drake again after so many months. Seeing a bathroom as we followed the others toward the auditioning room, I ducked inside. "Lana!" Dallas whined.

"You go on," I told her. "I just...I need a minute."

"Fine." She sighed and kept on walking.

It took me a while to get my nerves under control. I stood in front of the sink, staring at myself in the mirror. *Play it cool. Act as if you haven't been dying inside without him. He's still the same Drake. You can do this.*

The mental pep talk I gave myself calmed me for the most part. When Dallas sent me an annoyed text, I knew I couldn't hide any longer. I entered the audition room, keeping my eyes down so I didn't look at Drake before I was ready. He had always had this way of making me lose my mind with just a look, and I needed some more prep time before that happened.

114

When I dropped down beside Dallas in the last row she was pissed. "Do all rock stars think that they can snap their fingers and anyone with a vagina will drop their panties for them?" she asked.

I blinked, surprised at her question and the fire in her blue eyes. "Um...Yeah. You've met Shane. That's the way it works in their world." I knew that better than most. Vegas still haunted me.

"Pricks," she muttered.

"What did I miss?" I asked, half afraid of her answer.

If Drake had tried anything with Dallas I didn't know if I could sit there without having an emotional meltdown. She was my friend, but I was sure I would end up doing some physical damage to her pretty face!

"Axton Cage is a douche bag," she informed me, like I didn't already know that.

I had hung out with the "rock god" more than once. He wasn't the nicest guy, but he wasn't the worst one I had ever meet either. He was cool as long as he wasn't drinking or drooling over Gabriella Moreitti. But those two had broken up about six months ago, for good this time or so all the tabloids had reported. Gabriella wasn't a topic that we happily talked about in my family. Emmie and Gabriella had a war going on between them, and that meant Layla was anti-Gabriella as well. Which in turn, because I was loyal to my sister, meant that I was definitely anti-Gabriella!

"Oh shit! That's Lana!" Axton exclaimed. The sound of my name made my head snap around, and I was caught in the blue-gray gaze of Drake Stevenson.

My heart literally skipped a beat. He was my soul mate. I had always known that, and my soul had been without its mate for far too long. My skin felt as if it were going to split open from the emotions shooting through me. Drake looked good. Oh, fuck. He looked amazing. He had lost a little weight and there were a few new lines around his eyes and mouth.

His hair was a few inches longer, and I thought I saw a little gray at the corners, but to me he had never looked better.

My stomach tightened and lower, liquid heat pooled. My nipples hardened and I mentally chastised myself for not being able to control my physical reaction to the sight of the sexy rocker. No one had ever affected me like this but Drake.

As I took all of him in, I realized that I wanted him back in my life. On what terms I wasn't clear of yet. I didn't know if I could be his friend without falling deeper for him, but I wasn't sure if I wanted more from him. I just knew that I couldn't keep going on without him in my life.

A small smile tilted my lips as I came to that conclusion, and I raised my hand to wave. I thought I saw relief cross his face, and he started to smile back, but then he turned his head, frowning at something the man at the end of the judge's table had said...

That was when I saw him. Cole Steel. That was probably the biggest shock of my life. No way! I glanced at Dallas, but she didn't seem at all fazed about the old rocker's presence. Maybe it was because she wasn't easily impressed with superstars. Maybe it was because she was still pissed at Axton. Or maybe it was because she didn't know that dirt bag's secrets like I did!

Somehow, I contained my shock. Okay, I was beyond shocked, but no one needed to know it. They didn't have to know anything. If I kept my cool, then everything would be fine. Cole wouldn't know who I was, wouldn't even guess the truth. There was only one feature that we shared, and that wasn't all that big of a detail to notice.

"You're going to break your phone if you don't relax your hold on it," Dallas told me after a few minutes. "Is it that bad seeing him after so long?"

"Yes," I whispered, and then shook my head to clear the hatred haze. "No," I corrected myself, knowing that she had meant Drake and not Cole. "No. It's actually good to see him. I've missed him."

The sudden crash startled me, and I jumped up, not knowing what to expect. Drake had Cole pressed against the wall holding him up by his throat, and it scared the hell out of me. He was saying something to the older rocker, but it was too low for me to make out. His face was purple he was so mad, and there was a vein popping out in his neck.

Around me, the other fans were becoming rowdy. Axton was still sitting at the judge's table, seeming reluctant to stop his friend. A producer and two security guards appeared, attempting to pull Drake off of Cole, who was clawing at Drake's hands while he gasped for air he wasn't going to get.

I pushed passed Dallas, knocking another woman to the ground as I rushed toward the fight. If you could even call it that! It looked more like Drake dominating some little old man the way Cole Steel looked right now, still pressed against the wall.

"Drake!" I screamed his name as I ran toward him. He seemed to jerk at the sound of my voice but still didn't release his hold.

I glanced around, frantic. "Shane!" I screamed. "Shane!" Where was he? Before I could reach Drake strong arms wrapped around my waist. "No. Let me go!" I kicked behind me, connecting with someone's shins.

"Dammit, Lana!" Axton huffed. "Be still!"

"Let go, Ax. He's going to kill him." I had never seen so much rage coming from Drake before. "Let. GO!"

"Drake!" Shane's voice boomed around the room, and I glanced around, relieved to find the younger Stevenson brother. He reached his brother and wrapped his arms around his neck in a sleeper hold. "Let him go, bro."

Drake struggled as his brother pulled him back. "Fucker!" he bellowed. "You ever talk about her like that again and I will end you!"

117

Cole put his hands to his bruised throat, coughing as he sucked in life giving oxygen. Shane was still pulling Drake back, getting him as far away from the old man as possible while his brother struggled to get back. "A little help here, Ax!" Shane muttered, out of breath.

I was still trying to get free from Axton's hold on me. He seemed more eager for Drake to finish what he had started than keeping him back. "Sure. As soon as this little spitfire stops clawing at me, I'll be right there!"

I reached down and caught Axton off guard when I bit into his forearm. He released me with a string of curses, and I stumbled a few steps before righting myself. Then I was doing what I had meant to do in the first place. I threw myself against Drake.

He went completely still in his brother's arms. There was only a small hesitation and then he was wrapping me in his arms. I felt his nose skim against my neck as he inhaled deep. Drake's big body shuddered, and I thrust my fingers through his hair, holding him in place as the rage faded.

Shane released his brother. "Why didn't you just let her go in the first place?" Shane demanded, glaring at Axton. "She could have had this whole fucking thing taken care of in five seconds flat."

Axton shrugged. "Maybe I didn't want her to stop it. Fucker had it coming to him." Calmly, as if nothing had just happened, he dropped down in his chair once more and pulled out his phone.

Behind me the producers and staff were going crazy. Someone kept asking Cole if he was okay. The group of fans was shown out and someone was demanding to know what was going on. I was only half-aware of it all happening, too lost in the exhilaration of being in Drake's arms for the first time in forever.

"Give me one good reason why I shouldn't have you tossed in jail?" Someone demanded, stopping behind Drake.

I raised my head to find a fifty-something man with a receding hairline and a big belly glaring at Drake's back. "Do you think that just because you're some rock star you can act the way you want and get by with it?"

"Do you think fuck-face can talk about his family like that and he would let it pass?" Axton commented from his chair. "Nah, man. Steel was asking for it and he knew it. If he wants to be a pussy about it, then he doesn't need to be on the same stage as me and Stevenson."

I raised a brow at the big bellied man. "You had to know what you were getting into when you decided to do a reality show with rockers. They aren't exactly sunshine and daisies. Things are going to get hardcore around here. But that's what you wanted, right? Hardcore brings in the ratings."

"Just who the hell are you?" the man demanded. "You seemed to have caused all of this!"

Drake finally raised his head, turning a glare so cold on the man that he actually stepped back. "She's none of your fucking business," Drake said. "Do you understand?"

Instead of answering, the old man turned to check on Cole. "Are you able to continue?"

He was still coughing a little, but there was a grin on his face. "Reminds me of the good ol' days." Cole laughed. "Yeah, man. I'm good." His gaze went to Drake, and he held up his hands. "Peace. Lesson learned and all that shit."

"Then let's get back to work!" Big Belly clapped his hands. "Get this place cleaned up and show another group of fans in." He glanced back at me. "Will you be staying?"

I shrugged. "For a while." I wasn't about to take off yet. "And my friend will be too." I glanced over at the door where Dallas was still standing, having evaded the guards that had escorted the others out. She looked bored and was still texting away on her cell like nothing had happened.

"Get them some passes," Big Belly told an assistant who rushed to do his bidding.

"Well, that was fun." Shane sighed as he straightened the turned over chair his brother had left behind when he lunged at Cole. "Hey, Dray. Did you see the way Ax was holding Lana? Want to break his finger?"

"Whoa, bro!" Axton held up his hands. "Do you not see my arm? I think I need a rabies shot!"

I felt Drake tense at first, and then he buried his face in my hair again, his shoulders shaking as he tried to contain his laughter. "You bit him?"

A grin teased my lips. "Yeah. Pretty hard too."

Strong arms tightened around my waist. "Good job," he muttered, warm lips skimming across the sensitive skin below my ear, and I couldn't contain my shiver. It surprised me that he kissed me, and I wasn't sure how I felt about it...

Sure, my heart was beating like crazy, and my body was aching for him, but I didn't know if I was ready—if I would ever be ready—for Drake. With reluctance, I stepped back. "Are you okay now?"

"I haven't been okay for seven months," he said, his blue-gray eyes intent on my face. "But yeah, I'm good now."

I swallowed hard and took another step back, needing the added space between us. A glance behind me showed me that Dallas was getting bored with her phone. She was watching me, and I waved her over. "Dallas, come meet Drake," I told her, and she gave him one of her killer smiles.

He shook her hand when she reached us. "Hello, Dallas."

"Dallas is one of my roommates and the current foul mouth in my life." I grinned when Dallas flipped me off. "See?"

"Hey, Lana!" Axton called from his seat. "Introduce us."

I shot him a sour look. "I heard that you already introduced yourself, Ax. Do yourself a favor and put in some effort, dumbass."

His brows rose at that. "Effort? What is this 'effort' you speak of?"

Chapter 14

Drake

The instant the words were out of his mouth I saw red.

Rage didn't even begin to explain what I was feeling when the old rocker insinuated that Lana was part of the Hos-R-Us club that were typical groupies. My vision became tunneled; all I saw was that fucker, and I went in for the kill. Jumping up so fast that my chair fell over, I didn't notice that Axton ducked out of the way so I had better access.

I grasped his throat and pushed until the wall stopped me. Cole's head made a loud THUNK sound as it cracked against the stone wall.

"Don't you fucking talk about her like that!" I growled. "She's mine!" He wheezed as I tightened my hold around his neck. "Don't say another word about her. Don't even fucking look at her!"

Someone tried to pull me back, but I shrugged them off. "Lana deserves respect and she will have it."

"Drake!" I stilled when I heard my name from the only source that mattered, but it didn't completely clear the red from my eyes.

"Shane!" she screamed. "Shane!" I dimly heard from behind me.

Strong arms wrapped around my left arm and neck. I struggled as my brother pulled me away from Cole Steel.

"What the fuck are you doing, Drake?" he muttered in my ear as he kept pulling me backward. "Let him go, bro.

I struggled harder. "Fucker! You ever talk about her like that again and I will end you!"

"A little help here, Axton."

I heard the other man say something and then shout as if he was in pain. The next thing I knew, all was right in the world—at least in my world—when gentle arms wrapped around me. It surprised me so much I didn't believe it was happening at first. Then I realized I didn't care if it was really happening or not, just that I could feel her. I pulled her closer and buried my face in her hair.

Sweet Jesus! She smelled so good. Just like I remembered, the subtle scents of her shampoo and lotion. Her skin was warm and soft under my nose as I skimmed it back and forth. I shuddered, not sure if I could survive if it turned out that this was all in my head. I had dreamed of holding her in my arms, had fantasized about what I would do if I were ever graced with the chance. I heard voices, background noise, but nothing registered. I blocked it all out and focused on the only thing that mattered. Lana fit so perfectly against me. The way her full breasts pressed against my chest, delicate woman against hard male.

Her chest vibrated ever so slightly as she said something, and I turned my head to find the network's bigwig standing behind me with a scowl on his face. "Just who the hell are you?" The man demanded. "You seemed to have caused all of this!"

"She's none of your fucking business," I growled at him. "Do you understand?"

Things around us were calming down, and I pulled her back into my arms, not caring about anything else. Cole laughed off the incident, apologizing. I could see the way his eyes were still narrowed. I ignored him and everything else, burying my face in Lana's hair again. I wished I could bottle up her sweet smell and carry it around with me everywhere.

It was too tempting to resist, and I wasn't strong enough to even try. My lips brushed across her neck, just under her ear, and I felt her shiver. My cock was rock hard, and I was already thinking of some viable excuse to get us out of there and back to my apartment...

In the next instance she was pulling away. I saw the indecision in her whiskey colored eyes and realized that I had

122

a lot of work to do before she was truly back in my arms again. I was up for the challenge. She was worth it.

She introduced me to one of her roommates, the girl that Axton had been so into earlier. Dallas was gorgeous, with that dimple in her right cheek that peeked at you when she smiled. Her body was long and slender, and on closer inspection, inked up! Her tee shirt hid most of the ink, but some of it flashed me from time to time.

Shane came over and draped his arm around Lana's shoulders. "Dallas just got out of the modeling business," he informed me. "She thinks that just because she's all badassed up with her ink that no one would be interested in her for jobs."

I tried not to let my brother touching my girl bother me as I turned my attention on the blonde. "I'm sure Emmie could find her something if she were really interested in it."

Dallas wrinkled her nose. "No thanks. I'd rather slit my wrists than get back into modeling. It would only make my mother happy, and I try not to give her that satisfaction."

Lana grinned. "But just think, Dallas. What if you were in some hardcore rock video? Your mother would freak out!" Her eyes sparkled. "Oh! Oh! I know! I'll call Emmie and see if she knows anyone that needs a girl for their video! You can be in some rocker's bed in nothing but a smile! Your mom is going to have a stroke!"

"Don't call Emmie!" Axton called from his seat where he was still on his phone. "I'll hire her for OtherWorld's new video."

Dallas had seemed interested up until Axton had offered her the job. "Um, no." She rolled her eyes then glanced at her watch. "Lana, I have to go. Are you coming?" She glanced from Lana to me then back to Lana. "Or..?"

Lana sighed. "Yeah, I'm coming. I have practice at three."

My heart turned to lead. I didn't want her to go. Not yet. Not ever, dammit! She was already hugging Shane goodbye. I knew that I had to get back to work. We were holding up the tryouts, but I didn't give a fuck. I wanted more time with my angel.

Stepping back from Shane, she gave me a small smile. "It was really good seeing you, Drake," she murmured.

I pulled her into my arms, holding on tight for a moment before reluctantly releasing her. "Can we have dinner?"

She bit her lip and seemed to think about it before nodding. "When?"

"Tonight?" Lana nodded again and I felt some of the weight on my chest ease up. "I'll pick you up at seven."

She hesitated. "Um...I'll meet you there. Text me the place." She didn't give me time to protest as she grabbed Dallas by the elbow and pulled her toward the door.

I watched her go, frowning at her hasty exit. "I don't have your number..." She had changed it not long after she had gotten to New York. I knew because I had tried it on more than one occasion.

She paused at the door and glanced back. With a frown she pulled her phone from her hip pocket and messed with a few buttons. Seconds later my phone buzzed. "Now you have it!" she called back.

Lana

I was ten minutes late getting to the gym. I thought for sure Linc was going to blow a gasket. Instead, he just glared at me and rushed me through my stretches. My mind was only half on what I was doing. Thoughts of Drake kept haunting me.

I was anxious about dinner, worried about how I was going to deal with him while we shared a meal. Could I possibly fall back into the old routine that we had once had? I didn't know if I could. My feelings were too raw, my heart too fragile. Today had only shown me that I was still crazy in love with him, that it wouldn't take much before I was begging him to love me too...

124

Before I was begging him to make love to me!

"What is wrong with you?"

I blinked up at Linc, startled by his vehemence. "What? What did I do?" I hadn't been paying attention. We had been dancing for a while now and I had been on autopilot.

"Get your head out of the clouds, Lana," he scolded. "We have five weeks before the competition and you are dancing like some marionette with a broken leg!"

I grimaced. "Okay. Okay. I'm sorry." I sighed. "I'm focused now. Let's go again."

When I had first gotten to New York I had turned to dance to keep my mind occupied. I had started taking some jazz dance classes and found that I was kind of good at it. Then two months ago my teacher had asked if I wanted to compete since one of the couples in her team had backed out after breaking up. At first I hadn't wanted to, but after talking about it with my roommates, Linc had talked me into it, promising to be my partner.

For a big, hulky man he could dance like a freaking dream!

He took competing seriously though and made me practice three to four times a week. There were days when I wanted to throw him out the window of the private classroom that he reserved for us at the gym where he worked at.

"From the beginning." He hit a button on the remote to start the trio of songs that we planned on dancing to and pulled me into his arms.

Michael Bublé's *Sway* filled the room, and I let him lead me through the moves. I pushed all thoughts of Drake from my mind for the moment and let the music fill my soul as Linc spun and dipped me. When the song ended, *Save The Last Dance For Me* began, and I was smiling as the tempo became more upbeat.

By the end of the next hour, I was sweating and breathing hard, having just danced my ass off. I grabbed my stuff, blew Linc a kiss, and hurried home. He still had a few hours to go before his shift was over. He was a personal trainer and made a good bit of his money catering to the spoiled rich older women who came in just to ogle him for half an hour at a time.

If I was going to have dinner with Drake, I needed to plan what I was going to wear...and at least attempt to get a good hold on my emotions before I saw him again!

It was just after six when I finished putting on my makeup and looked down to find Drake's name flash across my screen followed by his text. I still had his number, had tortured myself by putting it in my new phone when I had gotten it. A few times over the last few months, I had come so close to texting him, but then Vegas would come back to haunt me.

I had forgiven Drake for that night almost immediately, but it wasn't something that I would ever be able to forget...

Picking up my phone and my clutch, I hurried out of the bathroom I shared with Harper. She was sitting in the living room with her computer on her lap going over the pictures she had taken earlier that day. She waved at me as I headed for the front door. "Be safe. Got your mace?"

I held up my clutch. "Got it!" I blew her a kiss as I ran out the door.

Forty-five minutes later, my taxi pulled up outside of the restaurant that Drake had texted me to meet him at. I was running late and hadn't even had time to mentally coach myself on how to deal with tonight. As I stepped out of the taxi, I frowned at the ritzy establishment. What was it with the members of Demon's Wings and wanting to take me to these places?

I clenched my jaw. Jesse had taken me to a place much like this when he had been in New York. I had understood his reasons. He had been thinking more about Layla than me at the time, wanting her to have the experience of a high-end dinner in one of New York's exclusive restaurants.

With Drake... He knew that I didn't like places like this. The food was always too rich, the cost always too extreme. He knew that I would rather have a pizza or a cheeseburger at a fast food place. It was crazy, but I was hurt that he wanted to have dinner with me here.

Had he completely forgotten what I was like?

When I entered the restaurant I found that I was underdressed compared to some of the patrons. My dress was simple, silver in color, an ended about mid-thigh. It wasn't cheap, but it in no way compared to the dresses on some of the other women, who were also decked out in thousands of dollars of diamonds.

The hostess offered me a forced smile, as if she knew I didn't belong there. "May I help you?"

I raised my chin, refusing to let this woman with her fake smile and even faker tan, make me feel unworthy. "Yes. I'm meeting Drake Stevenson."

Her eyes widened and she stepped forward. "He's already seated. This way please, Miss Daniels."

I blinked, having not expected her to know my name. I followed her through the dining room. A few heads turned my way, but I ignored them all as I kept my eyes on the back of the hostess' head. I didn't want to be here!

Drake was seated at a table in the back, hidden from most of the other diners. He stood as I drew closer and I took in his suit. Good God, that man was devastating in a suit! The way it encased all those wonderful muscles... I remembered to close my mouth so I didn't embarrass myself by drooling.

The hostess excused herself a few feet from Drake's table, and I stopped. As if sensing my hesitation, he stepped forward and pulled me against him.

"Are you okay?" he murmured against my hair.

I closed my eyes, fighting irrational tears. A hot rock star wanted to have dinner with me at one of Manhattan's most talked about restaurants and I wasn't happy about it. Maybe I needed to be medicated...but that still didn't stop my heart from hurting. Swallowing hard, I took a moment to get my emotions under control before stepping back.

"I'm fine," I told him with a smile that didn't reach my eyes.

"No you're not. I know you, Lana. Something's wrong."

"Apparently, you don't know me as well as you think," I muttered half under my breath as I took another step back and pulled out a chair at the table.

Drake dropped back down into his chair. "Are you mad at me?" he asked.

I sighed. "Yeah. I guess I am." There was no use lying about it. I was mad and hurt and an emotional crazy woman. "But it's not your fault. I'm just being my normal bitchy self."

Dark brows rose over blue-gray eyes. "Maybe if you told me why you're mad I can do something about it. I don't want to start our night off by fighting, Angel."

My entire body felt a jolt. I sucked in a deep breath. I hadn't realized how much I missed being called *Angel* until right this instant. It felt good, so fucking good! "I don't want to fight either," I assured him when I could finally speak without crying. "Let's forget all about it and start over."

"That sounds good to me... After you tell me what's wrong." He reached for my hand and grasped it. Turning it over, he traced his fingers over my palm.

Oh. Fuck. ME! He needed to stop that or I wasn't going to have any resolve left tonight.

"I..."

"You..?" He smiled as if he knew what his touch was doing to me. Ah, hell! Drake's smile lit him up from the inside out.

"I hate that you asked me here!" I burst out while I still had the brain cells to do so. "You know that I loathe places like this. How many times have we sat and laughed at the ostentatious people who come to these places? I was looking forward to a night catching up with you, just being with you! Instead, we're here and it's like a stab in the heart." I bit my lip, looking away. "I'm crazy, I know. And a huge bitch. I should be thrilled that you wanted to bring me here. But I'm not. I'm fucking miserable!"

Drake was quiet. His fingers had stopped their pattern tracing on my palm. Slowly, I raised my head. The look in his eyes made my breath catch. He was eating me up with his gaze, and I didn't know what to do! He has never looked at me like that...Okay, once. He looked at me like that once, but that didn't count...

"I wanted to make tonight special. Show you how special you are to me. I thought that bringing you here would help do that. It's supposed to be one of the most romantic restaurants in the city." He released my hand and pulled his wallet out of his pocket. Tossing a few big bills on the table he stood, and grasping my hand once more, pulled me toward the door.

I was speechless as he pushed open the door and pulled me out onto the street. Minutes later, we were in a taxi heading toward his apartment. I didn't say anything, and he was busy on his cell ordering Chinese. Then he was talking to Shane. "I don't care where you go. Just don't fucking be there when we get home."

A happy grin teased at my lips and I sat back. I wasn't spoiled. Nope, not even a little!

"What's that smile for?" Drake murmured as he put his phone back in his pocket.

I shrugged. "Sorry. I was just thinking I am a spoiled bitch."

He grinned. "Yeah, you really are."

Chapter 15
Drake
What was I thinking?

I had wanted to show Lana that I had changed. That this time, things were going to be different. I didn't want to be just friends. I wanted it all! A romantic restaurant had been my big idea to show her that. I should have known that Lana wouldn't like it.

I was surprised that she didn't laugh in my face. I knew that she hated those kinds of places. All I had ended up doing was hurting her. I was such an idiot.

Now, as we sat on the floor in the living room, the television on some mindless movie that I was sure I had watched with her before, I felt at peace. How had I lived without her for so long? How could I live without her now?

She was laughing at something that was happening on the movie, eating beef broccoli with her chopsticks. Her hair fell over her shoulders and her dress was riding up her thighs, showing me her slightly golden legs. She was relaxed, enjoying our time together. It was almost like old times…

But this time I wasn't going to let her slip through my fingers. She loved me once…Did she still? I was too much of a coward to ask. Dropping my chopsticks into my carton of noodles and chicken, I set them aside and turned to face her. "Lana…"

"Hmm?" she murmured without looking at me.

"I've missed you," I confessed.

She pushed her food away and turned so she faced me. "I have missed you too, Drake."

I cupped her face in my hands. "I…Rehab was bad. I nearly gave up a few times." More than a few times, but there was only one thing that kept me going…"All I could think about was you. When I wanted to give up I would reach for my sketch pad and start drawing. Only when you were staring back at me did the need to give up ease."

She swallowed hard. "I'm glad you kept going. When Shane told me you checked yourself in, I was so proud of you. That you're still going strong..."

"It gets hard." Fuck, did it get hard! I had nights when I literally shook with the need for a drink. Those nights felt like they lasted for days instead of hours. I had learned that those were the nights I needed a meeting. I needed to talk through my urge. Shane had helped me, going to the meetings, showing support when I didn't feel like I deserved it.

"You've come a long way, babe." She smiled. "I'm happy for you."

"Can you forgive me, Angel?" I needed to know. If she couldn't then there was no hope for our future, but if by some miracle she could... "Can you forgive me for what I did?"

Lana leaned forward, her hands covering mine. "I forgave you a long time ago, Drake. Maybe even as soon as it happened." Her smile was sad. "I loved you. I would have forgiven you for anything."

Loved? I hated the past tense of that word. I was determined to make her love me again. Fuck, it hadn't been hard to make her fall in love with me the first time. If I actually worked at it this time...

My fingers shook as I pulled her closer. She came willingly and I took hope from that. Lana climbed onto my lap, and I just buried my face in her neck. Holding her like this was pure heaven, but the scent of her was driving me crazy. My lips developed a will of their own, and I kissed a trail from just under her ear to her collar bone.

A small whimper escaped her and her fingers clutched at my hair. "Drake...What are you doing?" She breathed.

I smiled against the pulse throbbing at the base of her throat. "Showing you how much I have missed you, Angel... Should I stop?"

"No…Yes… NO!" She tugged on my hair until my head was tilted back far enough for our eyes to meet. "Don't stop, Drake," she whispered before her lips covered my own.

The first taste of Lana on my tongue was mind blowing. I don't think I have ever tasted anything so sweet. I thrust my tongue into her mouth, exploring her further. She sighed with delight and sucked my tongue deeper.

I was unable to keep my hands still. My left wrapped itself in her hair, holding her head at the angle I wanted. The other skimmed down her bare arm, across her hip, and between her silken thighs. Her skin was so soft, so perfect. Without actually realizing that I was doing it, my fingers traced the edge of her panties.

She pulled back, breaking the kiss. "Wait." Her breathing was labored. "I… Just wait." She pushed her hair away from her face. "I need to think."

My fingers were still playing with her panties. "I've waited a lifetime," I told her as her heat scalded my fingertips. "But if you want to go slower I will." I wasn't going to rush this. If she needed more time before I made love to her, then I would give it to her.

Lana

His kiss was drugging.

I probably shouldn't have let him kiss me in the first place, but once those sinful lips touched mine, I was gone. Who was I kidding anyway? I knew what I had wanted the instant he had pulled me out of that stupid restaurant. All through dinner I kept feeling his eyes on me and knew—even if it was mostly unconsciously—that he wanted me just as much as I wanted him.

When I felt his fingers playing close to a place that had only ever been touched by one man, I got scared. Not because I was unsure if I was ready, or if this was what I wanted because if—no, when!—I made love with Drake, he would know that I had lied to him.

"Do you want me to stop?" he murmured, watching me closely.

I shook my head. "No... Just slow down." I swallowed my nervousness and lowered my head to his again. His lips were damp from our first kiss. I sucked his bottom lip into my mouth, delighting in his taste.

His hand released my hair and cupped my breast. My nipples hardened to the point of pain, my breasts swelling. Between my legs, his fingers continued to explore the edge of my panties. Just as his middle finger ventured underneath I decided that I would deal with the consequences of my lie later. For now, I needed Drake far too much to care about anything else.

I shifted, opening my legs more so he had full access to my pussy. He groaned as he pulled my underwear to the side and skimmed his fingers down the outer lips. I was wet, almost drenched with my liquid desire for this man. "God! Angel, your heat almost hurts..."

I buried my face in his chest, unable to contain my pleasure filled cries as he pushed down on my throbbing clit. My fingers twisted in his shirt, holding on tight as he took me higher with ease. My body began to shake as my climax rushed up on me.

"Drake!" I cried as he pinched my clit and tugged.

Just as I neared the edge he stopped. My head shot up, unable to comprehend why he had stopped right when I was about to come. "Wh..?"

"Shhh." He brushed a kiss over my lips and reached for the hem of my dress. "I need to see all of you."

With shaking fingers I helped him. My dress was tossed over the couch, and I worked on the clasp to my bra while he tugged my panties down my thighs. His eyes were on fire as he looked down at me. Shaking fingers traced across my

133

tattoo along my panty line. The words were written in beautiful cursive script and read: *Love Me Without Regret*.

"So fucking beautiful!" He growled.

Strong hands gripped my hips, and he lifted me until my back hit the cushions of the couch. Drake moved until he was on his knees between my spread legs. His eyes lingered on my pussy, seemingly entranced by it. I was still hanging on the edge, needing to come so badly I was shaking from it. While he continued to look down at me, I skimmed my fingers down until I touched my soaked lips.

"Oh, fuck!" he muttered as he watched me touch myself. "Dip them inside, Angel," he commanded in a voice so rough with desire it was almost demonic.

I thrust two fingers deep inside with ease, moaning at how good it felt. I was close, my inner muscles clutching at my fingers as I neared the end. With a growl, Drake pulled my hand away and sucked my fingers into his mouth. I watched in a desire filled daze as he sucked my arousal from my fingers.

Then his mouth was on my clit, making me scream with pleasure as he sucked it hard. I tossed my head back against the couch, shuddering as I tried to hold back. My fingers tangled in his hair as I lifted my hips and ground against his tongue. His hands cupped my breasts, holding onto me as I drove toward my orgasm.

"Fuck!" He groaned, tonguing me deeper. "You have the sweetest pussy I have ever tasted," he muttered. "Come for me, Lana. Come for me, my angel."

I was right on the edge, so close and yet unable to go any further. I wanted this so badly, but I needed more. "Please, Drake," I cried. "Please!" I wasn't even sure what I was pleading with him for. If I knew what it was that I needed to make me fall over the edge, I would be doing it right now...

Two fingers thrust into me deep, stretching me. Sharp teeth bit into my swollen clit, and I screamed as I shattered into a million pieces. Drake lifted his head, and I met his gaze, letting him see my expression as I continued to convulse around his fingers as they thrust in and out of me.

When I lay there spent from the force of my orgasm, he climbed onto the couch with me and pulled me close. I could feel his erection pulsing against my thigh but was unable to do more than snuggle deeper against him for the moment.

"Rest, Angel," he whispered, kissing my temple.

I closed my eyes, fighting a yawn. He felt so warm, so safe. I gave up the fight and drifted off...

Drake

Watching Lana sleep was one of my favorite things to do. She was asleep because I had given her such a powerful orgasm, and that made me both smug and content.

I took her all in, every breathtaking bare inch of her. Her skin tone was a little darker than my own from her summer tan, making a mesmerizing contrast to my own lighter complexion. Her high breasts rose with each small inhale that she took. Her stomach muscles seemed to quiver with each exhale. I wanted to trace the dip that led to her belly button but didn't want to chance waking her. Lower her ink stood out against her honey kissed skin. The tat was done in curvy script and the words almost mocked me as I read them.

Love Me Without Regret

I did. I loved her and I didn't regret it. I never would!

For an hour, I just sat there on the couch watching her as she lay pressed against me. But then my erection became painful, and I shifted, trying to ease some of the pressure building in my balls. My movement woke her. Whiskey colored eyes opened, and I lost myself in their rich depths. Slender fingers cupped my jaw, tracing across the stubble.

"Am I dreaming?" she murmured.

I grinned. "If you are, then I hope you never wake up."

She bit her lip. "Drake, I'm naked." I nodded. Yes, she was gloriously naked, and I was feasting my eyes on every inch of her nakedness. "But you still have all your clothes on... Something's wrong with that picture, babe."

Laughing, I shifted until she was under me and started unbuttoning my shirt. "Then let's fix it." I got half way down before I gave up and tore the shirt off instead. Buttons went flying and Lana giggled. I dropped a kiss on her lips, loving the sound of her bell like giggles. "Unbuckle my belt," I commanded when I sat back on my knees.

Her fingers skimmed across my fly, and I nearly blew apart at the innocent touch. With trembling hands, she undid my belt and then the top button on my pants. My erection was so stiff it pushed the zipper down before she could reach for it. As her gaze fell on my dick, I watched her eyes darken.

"Do you like it?" I questioned as her fingers brushed over the tip.

"It's breathtaking," she whispered. "Will you let me suck it?"

I groaned as her question made my mind fill with all kinds of images. "I want you to, but I don't think I will last if you do." I stood and pulled the rest of my clothes off.

Standing there naked before Lana, I felt as it were my first time. Maybe because this was the first time with someone that mattered. Or maybe it was because this was the very first time I would be making love instead of just fucking some random girl.

Lana moved so fast I didn't have time to think as her hands grasped my cock. I saw her head move but was too dazed to realize what she was doing until her mouth slid down my length. My knees nearly buckled from the sheer pleasure of her sinfully hot mouth taking me in. She gagged as the head of my cock hit the back of her throat, but she didn't stop. Instead, she worked me until she was able to set a rhythm so she could breathe through her nose.

"Angel!" My fingers tangled in her hair, holding her head in place as I thrust deep into her mouth. Her mouth stretched around me, and her eyes glazed as she tried to take me deeper with each thrust I gave her. She raised her eyes, capturing my gaze and I was lost. Having her watch me with those whiskey eyes of hers while she sucked my dick deep down her throat was too much for me.

"Fuck! Angel, I'm coming."

Her eyes never left mine as the first hot stream hit the back of her throat. She kept sucking, taking all of me. She swallowed most of it, but some spilled from the sides of her mouth and dripped down her chin. I had never seen anything so mind-blowingly sexy in my fucking life as my come spilling from Lana's mouth like that.

As the last drop left me, I pulled free and fell to my knees, unable to support my own weight a moment more. Lana's arms wrapped around my neck and I buried my face in her bare chest as my body shook from the force of my release.

How long we stayed like that I couldn't say. The air conditioning against our bare skin made us both shiver, and I finally raised my head. Lana pushed my hair away from my face.

"I've always wanted to do that," she confessed with a devilish twinkle in her eyes.

I pulled her closer. "Angel, you can do that as often as you want," I promised as I stood and lifted her into my arms. Her arms wrapped around my neck as I carried her toward my bedroom.

My room was a mess: clothes tossed everywhere, empty soda cans here and there. My favorite Fender was leaning against the bedside table, and there were half a dozen picks tossed on top of it. The bed wasn't even made. Lana didn't even blink at the sight of it all, used to the way I tended to live.

"I guess you don't have a maid." She grinned up at me as I tossed her on the bed. She bounced twice and squealed as I jumped down beside her as soon as she landed. "Guess you are really missing Layla."

I snorted. "I missed Layla as soon as she married Jesse. The new housekeeper that Emmie hired doesn't pick up the dirty clothes that your sister would." I reached for the covers tossed haphazardly across the bed and kicked my legs until they were straight enough to drape over the both of us.

She giggled. "Poor thing!"

"She's not as sweet as Layla either."

The new housekeeper was a forty-something woman that spent more time frowning than smiling. I tried to avoid her, because she didn't have the nicest of personalities. Emmie didn't like her, and I wondered why she had hired the woman, but I assumed it had something to do with the way she made every surface in the house shine and how clean she got everything. She didn't live in the guesthouse like Layla had simply because she had four kids and a husband that wouldn't fit in the one bedroom house.

Lana pressed her feet against my legs, and I jerked back. "Why are your feet always so cold?"

"Don't be such a baby." She snuggled closer and I suddenly didn't care that she had her icicle feet on me. Her head fit just right under my chin as she rested it on my chest. Midnight black hair spread over my shoulder and pillow and I ran my fingers through the ends, truly happy for what felt like the first time in my entire life.

138

Chapter 16
Lana

I woke with a warm man pressed up against my back. It took me a full minute before I realized I wasn't still dreaming. Then the night before came flooding in and I smiled, soaking in the reality.

Raising my head, I saw that it was just after seven from the digital clock beside the bed. Muttering a curse that would have had Layla scolding me for sure, I untangled myself from Drake's arms. He grumbled something in his sleep and tightened his arms around me for a moment before easing up enough for me to slip free.

My clothes were still in the living room, and I didn't know if Shane was home or not. So I picked up the first shirt I stumbled across and smelled it to make sure it didn't stink before slipping it over my head. You never knew with Drake sometimes. Without my sister around to do his laundry, I doubted if the shirt I was now wearing had seen the inside of a washer since he had moved in.

It didn't smell bad. If anything it smelled sexy as hell to me, with the scent of his body wash and deodorant still clinging to the fabric. The shirt fell just short of mid-thigh, and I left the bedroom in search of my clothes and the possibility of coffee.

My dress and underwear were still where Drake had tossed them the night before. His clothes spread across the floor spoke volumes to what had taken place. I couldn't help but smile a little as I slipped my panties on and headed for the kitchen. Last night had been amazing...

I stopped mid-stride when I noticed Shane standing in nothing but a pair of boxers in front of the open fridge. His hair was a mess and he needed a shave. The tattoos on his back and bare arms were sexy as hell, but I felt nothing as I watched him pull out a carton of milk and chug. When he was done, he put the milk back and turned around.

He took in my borrowed shirt and rumpled hair with a casual shrug as he wiped his milk-stash away with the back of his big hand. "Morning, sis."

"Hey... Got any coffee?" I didn't want things to be awkward. How many times had I seen Shane like this in the past? But never before had I just left his brother's bed after a night of really heavy foreplay.

"Sure. You want regular or Jesse's special recipe?" he asked as he pulled out the coffee beans from the freezer.

"Regular, please." I didn't think I could handle my brother-in-law's special recipe. Only once had I made the mistake of drinking his brew, and I hadn't slept for two days.

"You got it." He went about making the coffee then made us both a bowl of cereal.

"Drake up yet?" Shane asked as he shoveled a big spoonful of bran flakes and raisins into his mouth. "I think he's supposed to be at the studio at nine."

"He was still sleeping pretty soundly when I crawled out of bed." Shane raised a brow and I blushed, but he didn't say anything. "Should I wake him up?"

He grinned. "Yeah. You better be the one to do that. It might be more effective than if I did it."

I pushed my half eaten cereal away. "I have to get going soon anyway. I have to be at the gym at nine thirty, and I still need to get home and change."

"Then you better make it a quickie!" he called after me, and I shot him the finger without turning around.

My face was still warm when I walked into Drake's room. My rocker was spread out across the king sized bed. His tattoo was actually quivering with each breath he took while he clutched at his pillow. It took me only a moment to realize that he was in the middle of a bad dream.

A moan left him and I fell onto the bed, shaking his arm as he started to tremble. "Drake. Drake, wake up."

"No!" he shouted. "No... Shane. No!"

I cupped the side of his face. "Drake, baby, wake up. It's just a dream. Wake up and look at me!"

Blue-gray eyes snapped open, but I could tell his nightmare still lingered as the fear slowly faded from his eyes. "Angel?" he croaked.

"Yes. I'm here." I stroked my hand up and down his back soothingly. It was damp with sweat from his dream, but I didn't care. I knew about the reasons for the bad dreams, and I just wanted to comfort him until his mind eased.

He moved so fast I didn't have time to blink. One minute I was on the edge of the bed, rubbing his back, the next I was underneath him. His knees spread my thighs wide, and I gasped as the head of his dick teased at my pussy.

"I need you." He growled as his mouth captured mine.

All thoughts of either one of us being late disappeared at the first taste of his mouth. One big hand tangled in my hair while the other explored my body. A cry of pleasure escaped me as he pinched and pulled on my nipples. I could feel my pussy flooding with arousal even as the head of his dick rubbed across my opening.

Drake was wild in my arms, out of control as he made love to me. I didn't have time to think as he assaulted me with one pleasure after another. His mouth left mine to kiss a scalding trail down my neck and across my collar bone. That hot, sinful mouth sucked my nipple deep inside and I couldn't contain the small scream at the pleasure filled pain as he sucked me harder with each pull.

"I need you, Angel." He breathed against my stomach as his tongue dipped into my belly button.

"I need you too!" I cried as his tongue stabbed into my pussy. "Drake!"

"Such a sweet pussy." He sucked my clit into his mouth, nipping at the bundle of nerves. I twisted against his mouth, already on the edge of a mind numbing orgasm.

"Please. Drake, please!" I begged as his day old beard rubbed against my thighs, making the pleasure that much more intense.

His head rose and I could see the evidence of my arousal on his scruffy face. Those blue-gray eyes were so full of passion it made my breath catch.

"Tell me you want me," he demanded as he grasped his dick in his hand. I watched in complete fascination as he stroked the head of that big, beautiful cock down my clit.

My thighs trembled in anticipation. "I want you, Drake," I breathed. "Please, I need you inside of me."

I watched him position himself at my opening and swallowed hard at how beautiful this picture looked to me. Drake with his long, thick cock ready to become a part of me. His hair covered thighs pressed roughly against my tanned, smooth ones.

"Look at me!" he commanded and I raised my eyes until our gazes locked.

"You are mine, Angel." He made it sound like a vow as he thrust hard and deep.

The scream that escaped me was full of the most carnal pleasure. It had been so long, and I was tight. His thick cock stretched me almost to the point of pain, and I arched my hips in an attempt to ease some of the pressure. Drake's eyes were dilated until there was no blue-gray, only black.

"There is no better feeling," he growled.

"Drake..." I shifted my hips, urging him to move. "Please."

He pulled free then thrust deep and hard. I felt his balls bounce against my ass and wrapped myself around him to hold on while he drove into me over and over again. My thighs where shaking, burning with each powerful thrust as he hit that spot that always made me lose my mind for him.

"Angel!" he cried, and I could feel him growing thicker inside of me as he neared the end.

"Take me with you!" I pleaded, and his hand eased between us until his thumb found my clit. He pressed down hard and rubbed in tight little circles. "AH!" I screamed as my inner muscles started to contract around his engorged cock. "Drake, I'm coming!"

"Yes! Fuck, yes!" he bellowed just before his back arched and he emptied himself deep inside of me.

The feel of his hot release inside of me only intensified my orgasm. I clawed at his back as my climax went on and on, until I thought I was going to pass out from the sheer pleasure of it all...

Drake lay on top of me, sweat coating both of our skins. His face was against my neck, his lips kissing the sensitive spot just under my ear. I was spent and still floating on a euphoria cloud. I didn't want this moment to ever end. Fuck the world because I wasn't ready to leave this bed or this man.

There was a slight tab on the closed door. "Lana?"

Drake's head jerked up. "Go the fuck away, Shane!" he roared.

"Sorry, bro." Shane called through the door. "I hate bothering you guys, but Lana's phone keeps ringing. It's Layla and she keeps calling. It might be important."

My heart stuttered in my chest. "I'll be right there!"

Drake's arms tightened around my for a moment before he muttered a curse and rolled off. "Come back," he commanded, pulling the covers over his waist as I pulled on the shirt that he had stripped me of without even knowing it. Instead of putting on my wet panties, I grabbed a pair of boxers from his dresser and stepped into them as I headed for the door.

When I opened the bedroom door Shane was standing there, my phone in his hand. "Sorry, sis." He grimaced.

"It's okay." I gave him a small smile as I took the phone from him. A glance at the screen told me that I had five missed calls. Heart pounding, I pulled up my sister's number and hit connect.

It didn't even finish ringing once before Layla answered. "Oh, God! Are you okay?" she asked.

Something in my sister's voice told me that she was upset. "I'm fine. What's wrong?"

"I didn't know!" she cried. "I had no idea. If I had, I never would have let Drake accept the job. Please believe that."

I went still. "Layla..."

"I couldn't believe it when Jesse told me that he was one of the judges. I'm still in denial!" She went on as if she hadn't heard me.

I glanced over at the bed and pulled the phone away from my ear. "I...I'm going to take this in the bathroom." I told him and rushed through the open bathroom door before he could protest. When I was alone, I locked the door and turned on the faucet. "Layla, are you still there?"

"Lana what's going on?"

"I...I'm at Drake's," I whispered. "I don't want to talk about this right now, Layla."

There was a long pause on the other end, and I could actually hear the wheels turning in her head. "Did you spend the night?"

"Yes." I wasn't going to lie to her about it. "But I'm about to leave. I have to meet Linc..." A glance at the clock on my phone showed me that I had forty minutes to get where I needed to be before he went ape-shit on my ass.

"Cole is the third judge, Lana. Did you know?"

I sighed. "Yeah. I found out yesterday when I stopped by to watch the auditions." I ran my fingers through my tangled hair, trying to get it to look at least a little less crazy sex-ish. "I saw him."

"And you're okay? Are you sure?" Layla sounded concerned now that she wasn't so frantic.

"I'm fine, Layla. He means nothing to me. Why would I be bothered by seeing him?" Okay, so maybe I had been a little bothered by seeing Cole Steel yesterday. That didn't mean I needed to burden my sister with that shit.

"Lana...Jesse knows. I had to tell him because I kind of freaked out when he told me last night. He's upset because I told him everything. He wants to come out there and see you. Maybe even punch Cole in the throat." I closed my eyes and rested my head against the tiled wall. "I'm sorry, Lana. I couldn't keep it from him."

"I understand. He's your husband, Layla. Of course you had to tell him." I dropped down on the closed toilet seat, rubbing at my suddenly aching head. "I don't think it's a good idea if you guys come out here. Drake doesn't know and I'm not ready to tell him about Cole. Jesse's too much of a hot head..."

"I don't know if I can keep him from going, but I will see what I can do, sweetheart. Maybe stall him until he's less volatile. He's seriously upset though, Lana. Jesse loves you."

Hot tears pricked my eyes, and I closed them to keep them from spilling out. "I love him too... I have to go, Layla."

"Okay, baby. I'll call you later... Tell Drake I said hi. I'm not sure if this is what you need right now, but I'm happy for you if this is what you want."

When I opened the door Drake was still where I had left him. He was frowning at the ceiling. "Layla says hi," I said with a small smile. I didn't want the conversation I had just had with my sister to affect the happiness that I had just minutes ago with the sexy man still lying on the bed.

"Is everything okay? Lucy?"

I shook my head. "Lucy is fine." My baby sister was beyond okay these days. Jesse and Layla had adopted her, making her officially their daughter. Lucy loved Jesse to death and had even started calling him "Dad" recently. I was happy for her.

She had the one thing that Layla and I had never had. A father that loved her. "And so are Layla and Jesse."

Drake raised a brow. "Then why the frantic calls?"

"She was just worried about me." Not a lie. I crossed back to the bed and dropped down on the edge. "You're going to be late for work."

He grunted. "Who cares? Cole's late every morning. My lateness isn't going to hurt anything." He reached for me and pulled me across his chest. "Let's stay in bed all day and make love until we can't walk."

I grinned, loving that idea, but Linc was going to seriously kill me if I didn't show up. "I would if I didn't have to meet my friend." He frowned and I rushed to explain why I had to go. "Linc..." his whole body tensed "...my very *gay* roommate, is my dance partner in this jazz dance competition that we're doing in a little over a month. I have to meet him at our gym for practice."

Drake relaxed. "Okay." He sighed. "I hate that you're going to leave me if for only a few hours... Why don't you come by the studio later and we can have lunch?"

"Will you behave?" I asked, only half teasing. The fight from yesterday still lingered in my mind. That had been scary as hell. I hated Cole, but I didn't necessarily want him dead!

He crossed his heart. "Promise."

I dropped a kiss on his lips. "Okay. I'll come by." Reluctantly, I stood. There wasn't time to go home and change. "Can I barrow some sweats?"

"Of course, but they will be too big. Ask Shane if he has anything. I'm sure he has a few things that will fit you."

I wrinkled my nose as at the idea. No way was I going to wear something that had come off of one of Shane's one-nighters. "Um, yeah. No thanks."

I crossed over to the dresser and pulled out a pair of sweats pants. He was right. They would be too big, but I could work with that. Grabbing a clean shirt from the next drawer, I headed for the shower.

Chapter 17

Drake

As the door closed behind Lana and I heard the faucet turn on, I frowned. Obviously, she didn't want me to know what she was saying to her sister. It didn't really bother me. I was sure she was just trying to explain why she hadn't answered her phone the first time Layla had called.

If I were Layla I would be worried too. Especially when she found out that her sister was sleeping with the man who had hurt her so badly back in December. Grimacing, I decided to call Layla and assure her that I only wanted to make Lana happy. This time I wasn't going to fuck it all up!

With that settled in my mind, I instead turned to other things...like reliving the most incredible experience in my life. Making love to Lana had been epic. Just thinking about how tight she had been, how incredibly hot and sweet she had been as I had thrust into her over and over again, made me hard to the point of pain...

Yet even as I basked in the remembered ecstasy, something kept nagging at me. Lana had been tight...but not a virgin. It shouldn't have bothered me. Fuck, she had every right in the world to explore her sexuality. I had given up the right to be her first when I had hurt her in Vegas.

Just because I didn't have the right to care, didn't mean that I didn't!

I had dreamed of being Lana's first. Of teaching her all about passion and lovemaking. It made my gut ache with some unknown pain knowing that I hadn't been the one to do any of those things. Muttering a curse, I punched the bed on either side of me and glared up at the ceiling.

This was just one more fuck up that I was responsible for...

When Lana came out of the bathroom, looking flushed and her eyes red as if she had been crying, I pushed all my unreasonable thoughts away. "Layla says hi," she murmured.

I had been worried that something was wrong with her sisters or my band brother, and I was relieved when she assured me that they were okay. Her need to leave bothered me, but her explanation eased some of my upset. I was happy that she had gotten back into dancing. I knew that it had been a passion of hers as a little girl.

When she grabbed my sweats and headed for the bathroom to shower I didn't stay in bed long. Whistling to myself, I followed her and stepped into the huge walk-in shower with her. Five shower heads were already beating down on her from all imaginable angles. Her back was turned to me and I wrapped my arms around her waist, pulling her against my already throbbing erection.

"We don't have time for this, babe," she murmured, but there was an almost purr quality to her voice. She wanted me just as badly as I wanted her despite our earlier session in bed.

I nipped her just under her left ear. "Showering together will save time," I argued as I pushed her front up against the tiled wall. From behind, I parted her thighs until my dick fit just right. Her opening was drenched with her arousal. Leaning forward, I nuzzled her neck with my nose. "No matter what, we will always have time for this."

Her arms wrapped around my neck, pulling me closer as she turned her head and met my lips. I kissed her deep, playing with her tongue as I lifted her just enough for the head of my dick to slip into her dark recesses. Her cry was drowned in my mouth as I pushed into her until I was balls deep.

"Slow and easy or hard and fast?" I asked as I felt her muscles start to contract around me. Just one thrust into that tight, sinfully hot pussy and she was ready to come for me.

"Fast," she panted. "Hard." She pressed her ass back against me, inviting me to take her any way I wanted. "Please, Drake."

Her plea was my undoing, and I clamped my hands tightly around her hips to keep her in place as I began to thrust into her with reckless abandon. I pounded into her only a half a dozen times before she was screaming my name. Her muscles convulsed around my dick as I sunk deep into her each time. It felt so good. So fucking *good*!

"Angel," I ground out as I lost what little control I had on myself and emptied deep within her…

--

I was forty-seven minutes late.

Cole and Axton were already seated at our table when I walked in. The producer shot me a hard look, but I ignored him. I was too happy, too content with the world at large to care about anything or anyone else. Humming softly to myself, I dropped down beside Axton at the judge's table.

My friend grinned as I thanked the assistant who sat the mug of coffee down in front of me. "Drake Stevenson smiling, humming happily. Thanking people… Wow! I don't think I have ever seen any of those things happen in the entire time I have known you. Does the lovely Lana have anything to do with this change in you, old friend?"

"She has everything to do with it." I couldn't help the goofy grin that spread across my face as I pulled the ever present itinerary closer.

"Good for you, dude. I'm glad to see you so happy." He turned to Cole. "I think he's going to marry that girl."

"The leggy blonde or the stacked brunette?" Cole asked, sounding both bored and interested at the same time. How the hell was that even possible? Yet he pulled it off.

I refused to let his question put a damper on my good mood. "The brunette," I told him. "And yeah, I am going to marry her. Not anytime soon, though." Lana still had college to finish. Marriage was a few years away for us.

Cole nodded as if understanding. "The brunette. She was dynamite. And that mouth! She was keeping up with that brother of yours, man. Good choice."

"Listen, man..." Axton put his phone down after typing a few words and hitting send "...can you do me a huge favor?"

I raised a brow at him. Axton never asked favors. He didn't need to. If he wanted or needed something he either took care of it himself or called his assistant to do it for him. Sometimes he even called Emmie if he needed something major done quick. "I don't know. Maybe."

"Lana said something yesterday and I really like the idea. That Dallas chick would be ideal for OtherWorld's new video. She's hot, inked, hot, feisty... Did I mention hot?" I rolled my eyes at him. "Can you talk to Lana? Get her to work on her friend and persuade her to do it? I'll make sure the pay is sweet."

"I'll talk to her," I promised. "But don't get your hopes up, man. Lana told me a little about her last night and she isn't exactly Miss Sunshine."

"Yeah, I figured that out yesterday." Axton grinned. "Jesus Christ! She's hot."

Cole snorted. "Man, we know. Not only do we have eyes, but you've told us like a hundred times."

Before either of us could comment, the producer's assistant started showing in hopefuls. The next two hours passed in a blur of tone deaf, off key, cry baby boredom. I spent more time checking my watch or phone then paying attention. Really, I sucked at this job, but I didn't care. It wasn't like I needed the money or anything. If they fired me—which I knew they wouldn't because they didn't want to piss Emmie off—then it wouldn't bother me in the least.

At one thirty, Lana texted me to let me know she was outside, and I stood up the second the latest hopeful finished his shaky voiced attempt at some original song that he had written himself. "No," I told him point blank.

"Dray? Where ya going?" Axton called after me.

"Lunch. Lana's waiting outside for me," I called over my shoulder.

"Awesome. More Lana." I heard his chair scrape against the floor as he stood. "No way, dude," he told the hopeful. "Wait up! I'm hungry too."

I muttered a curse under my breath. I wanted a quiet hour with Lana. Just her and me, and maybe a little day-old Chinese food after a quickie, but it didn't look like that was going to happen. Axton caught up with me before I reached the door, and Cole was quick to follow. "Sounds good to me," the old rocker said as he fell into step with me and Ax. "I always did enjoy some eye candy while I eat."

As soon as I saw her my heart stuttered in my chest. Would it always skip a beat when I saw that girl? I fucking hoped so! The smile on her beautiful face when she spotted me coming her way was breathtaking, and I pulled her into my arms, kissing her until she moaned.

"You look beautiful," I said as I glanced down at her simple jeans and tank. The sweats that she had left my place in that morning were not something I wanted my friend to see her in. Especially since they had been hanging off her, even after she had rolled, tucked, and gathered the extra fabric into rubber bands to make them fit better.

"Thanks." She kissed me again, quick and hard. "I'm starving, babe. Where are we eating." Her gaze went over my shoulder and I felt her stiffen. "I assume it will be the four of us..."

Axton pushed between us, hugging her. "Yep. I'm not turning down the chance to be with little Lana."

She wrinkled her nose at him. "Why do I like you again?"

"My charming personality? The sexy rock god persona?" He smacked a kiss against her cheek, and I had to grit my teeth before I said something I would regret.

Lana raised a dark brow. "Yeah... No, neither of those things."

Axton pouted. "But...But...You don't like me?" He grinned. "You know you do, sweetheart. You don't have a mean bone in that beautiful body."

"Mean? Maybe not. Bitchy, fuck yeah!" She hugged him before stepping back and putting her hand in mine. "And you, rock legend? Are you going to be joining us too?"

Cole shrugged. "It looks like it, beautiful. Might as well tag along. You wouldn't deprive an old man of some company for a mere meal, would you, sweetness?"

I felt tension in Lana, but she didn't look like she was upset. In fact, she was smiling at Cole. "No. I wouldn't dare do a thing like that."

Lana

What the fuck had I been thinking?

I should have told Cole, and probably Axton too, that I didn't want them coming. I had been doing nothing but thinking about Drake all morning, and I had hoped we could have something small at a quiet café or something. Instead, I had had a moment of insanity and a plan had formed.

We all got in the back of Axton's car, since it was the first one we came to. Axton gave his driver the address for some deli that he said he favored and we were off. I was stuck between Ax and Drake while Cole took up the seat across from us. I didn't mind that I was squished up against Drake. I would have been pressed there even if Axton wasn't crowding us.

A silence descended the back of the car and I started to feel tense. Not even Drake's hand tracing little swirls on my arm could fully distract me. Sighing, I broke the silence. "So, Cole... Are you married?"

Cole snorted. "Tried that once. It didn't work out too well."

I knew all about his one marriage. It had ended in a nasty divorce. That had been about twenty years ago, and Cole had had to shell out a big load of cash to keep his secrets a secret.

"How about kids? Got any of those?" I was surprised that my voice was so calm, that I was able to keep my smile in place for so long without my face breaking.

The old rocker shrugged. "One or two. Neither of which want anything to do with me."

"That's too bad," I murmured, offering some sympathy. It would look really bad if I suddenly started screeching at him. "Sons? Daughters? Both?"

"One of each. My son is in the movie business. His mother is an actress." Which meant that the son's mother was also Cole's ex-wife. "And my daughter... I haven't seen her since she was a baby. Fuck, I don't even know what her name is. Her mother was a real bitch."

I stiffened. He had to be lying. Had to! No way had he seen me when I was a baby. Layla would have told me that kind of thing. Unless... Maybe she didn't know? Crap, now I was going to have to call her and ask her if she knew about it. Layla was going to worry, and Jesse was going to get pissed. Then hot head Jesse was going to fly out to New York and all hell would break loose.

Because as soon as the tabloids found out that I was Cole Steel's daughter and the reason for his expensive breakup from his wife... Oh and that I was currently Drake Stevenson's girlfriend... I wasn't going to have a moment's peace.

Chapter 18

Lana

It seemed like I had just blinked my eyes and five weeks had gone by. Maybe it was because I was so happy. I had no free time with summer school, the beginning of the fall term, and dance practice with Linc.

If possible, I had lunch with Drake every day. The auditions were still going on with the end of the line nowhere in sight. People actually had backpacks full of food and drinks, and they had sleeping bags so they could camp out in the line. Of course when I showed up, the producer always started muttering under his breath and was quick to wrap things up so I was out of the way sooner rather than later. Axton and Cole had lunch with us several times. I enjoyed spending time with Axton. His sarcasm was amusing, his sexiness easy on the eyes. He was a good friend. Cole—I had mixed feelings about. I wanted to keep hating that old fucker, but he had actually chipped away at the ice around my heart where he was concerned.

Turned out Cole Steel wasn't all bad. He could be charming when he wanted to be. Don't get me wrong, I would always hate that bastard, but at least I didn't have to try as hard to hide that hate all the time. I hadn't asked Layla about what Cole had said. I didn't want to open that can of worms just yet. It was getting harder and harder to keep Jesse in LA with each passing day, and I didn't want to give him a reason to jump on a plane with my sisters.

Today was Friday and I had talked Dallas and Harper into going with me to have lunch with Drake and the guys. Shane had begged me all evening last night to bring Harper, refusing to leave Drake and me alone until I gave in. He had it bad. Harper wasn't falling for any of his usual tricks, which normally had women handing over their underwear and pleading for the rocker to give it to them hard.

If possible, Axton was worse than Shane. Drake had asked me to persuade Dallas to do the OtherWorld video. I had worked on her for three days before she had given in and accepted. You had to know how to push the right buttons with Dallas because she was stubborn as hell. Mostly, she had mommy issues and was a real daddy's girl. Lucky for me—and Axton—that Austin Bradshaw hated his ex-wife just as much as his daughter disliked her. One phone call and Austin was in New York telling Dallas to accept the job.

That had been two days ago. Dallas had called Axton and told him that she would do the video... *If* I did it with her. Sneaky bitch! Put on the spot, I had had to agree. She had been staring me down at the time daring me to say no. Drake hadn't liked the idea. When his manager had suggested that I be in Demon's Wings video last Thanksgiving, Drake and Jesse both had gone a little crazy.

The producer shut down the auditions as soon as he saw me, shooting me a frustrated look. I shot him a grin, not caring that I was interrupting his day. Drake had to eat and he hadn't had a day off in over a month. My presence was the only thing that got the producer dick wad to move his ass and make things happen at a faster pace.

"Lana's here," Axton told Drake.

Drake stood without looking up from his phone. He was frowning down at something and I could only assume it was a text from Emmie. I went to him, not wanting him to bump into anything in his attempt to reach me. Standing on tiptoe, I kissed his cheek.

"What are you reading?"

His eyes lifted to meet mine, and he raised a brow at me. "Jesse just sent me a really interesting text."

Dread filled my stomach. I could only imagine what my brother-in-law had to say. He had been chomping at the bit for a while now. The last time I had talked to him he had demanded I tell Drake, but I hadn't been ready. I still wasn't ready!

Muttering a curse, I glanced back at my friends. Shane had come out of the woodwork and was talking to Harper, making her laugh like always. The sparkle in his blue-gray eyes was something I had seen in Drake's eyes a lot. Harper was still oblivious to the fact that she quiet possibly had one of the sexiest rock stars in the world watching her with bated breath. The girl had no self-confidence at all when it came to guys!

A few feet away, Dallas was rolling her eyes at Axton as he leaned against the wall beside her. I was sure the steel support beams were going to melt he was turning up the wattage on his charm so high. Dallas wasn't having any of it. I would have laughed if I hadn't felt the tension pouring off the man beside of me.

Turning my gaze back to him, I bit my lip. "Are you mad at me?"

"I don't know," Drake told me honestly. "I keep wondering why you didn't tell me, Angel. Don't you trust me?"

"Of course I do!" I cupped his face, hating to see the hurt in his eyes. Damnit! I had put that pain there, and it tore my heart to pieces. "I trust you, Drake. I...I just didn't know how to handle it. I'm sorry."

"Let's get out of here," he muttered, pulling me close for a tight hug but not a kiss. Still holding me close to his side, he pulled me toward the exit. As we passed Shane, he leaned over and whispered something in his brother's ear.

Shane nodded. "Sure. No problem. Take all the time you need." His gaze landed on me. "See you later, sis. If you need me, call."

Tears filled my eyes. Did that mean that Drake was about to breakup with me? All I could do was nod and let Drake push me through the door. Once we were in the back seat of

Drake's car he didn't speak, not one word until the door to his apartment closed behind us.

I dropped down onto the edge of the couch, my head bowed to hide my tears. "I'm sorry," I whispered. "I wasn't ready to tell you."

"Cole Steel? How the hell did your mom get involved with Cole-fucking-Steel?" he demanded, pacing back and forth in front of the entertainment center.

Swallowing hard around the lump in my throat, I told him. "You know that my mom wasn't that great. She wanted to be a rock star's trophy. And if not a rock star then some rich guy's arm candy. She seduced Tommy Kirkman when she was sixteen, knowing that she would get pregnant...And seven years later, when the money that Tommy had shelled out to keep Layla a secret started to dwindle, she set out to do it all over again with another rocker. Steel Entrapment was the hugest thing in the rock world back then. Seducing Cole was no big feat. Everyone knew that he cheated on his wife regularly. And as long as he kept his dick clean, she didn't care how many groupies he fucked around with."

Drake paused from pacing, but I didn't raise my head to look at him. "So what happened once your mom got pregnant? Once she had you?"

"When Lydia confirmed her pregnancy, she called Cole's wife, who started divorce proceedings that same day. It was a nightmare and while I hadn't been born yet, Layla still had to live through it. When I was old enough to ask, she told me all of it."

Like how Cole's wife had married him before he had gotten big, so he had to split everything with her fifty-fifty. Since there would be proof of infidelity once I was born, she was able to petition for alimony as well. The threat of having to shell out big money for child support for two children, as well as an outlandish figure for alimony from a vindictive wife, had really pissed Cole off. When I was born he had to be court ordered to take the paternity test. When it came back positive he refused to believe them and demanded another one done. This happened three more times before the judge stepped in and took over, making Cole pay up.

"When it was all over Cole was nearly broke," I told Drake as I wiped my damp eyes. "He hated my mother for it because really it was her fault. His son was ten and hated him because he had supposedly broken his mother's heart."

"And what made you hate him, Lana?"

I flinched, hating for him to call me by my given name. I was his "Angel," not Lana! "Cole didn't ride in and save Layla and me from the big bad gorgon. I hoped that my dad would want me. Love me. But he didn't. He was even given the chance of custody, but he turned it down. I read the court records. He said he 'Didn't want the bastard that had ruined his life.' So I decided that if he didn't want me, hated me for causing all his problems, then the feeling was going to be mutual."

"How old were you when you found out?"

"Seven, almost eight." I pushed my hair away from my face but still didn't look at Drake. "After that, I started listening for him on entertainment news, and if I saw his face on a magazine I always read it. He was all talk about how he wanted to reconcile with his son, but never once did he mention the daughter he had thrown away...

"A few years ago, right before my mom died, I got a certified letter meant for her saying that the child support was going to be cut off. The lab that had done the paternity tests was under investigation and for the support to continue, I had to show up for another DNA test." I grimaced. "I tore the letter up before Mom could see it. I didn't care if she got mad, but I wasn't going to go through with the test. Not willingly. Screw the child support checks; it wasn't like I saw any of that money anyway."

Drake crouched down in front of me and with a finger under my chin made me meet his eyes. "Don't cry, Angel," he murmured, wiping a few of my tears away with one of his thumbs. "You don't ever have to cry over your dad again."

"I really am sorry, Drake," I whispered. "I..."

"Shhh. I understand." He kissed my lips tenderly. "Just don't keep things like this from me again. I hate having secrets between us. Promise me we won't have any more."

"I promise!" I kissed him back, wanting more than just a gentle brush of his lips across mine. "Tell me we're okay, Drake. Swear that you aren't going to breakup with me."

"Is that what you thought?" He sighed, leaning his forehead against mine. "I can't live without you, Angel. I love you."

Those words were something I had been aching to hear almost from the first day I had met this man, yet I wasn't ready to repeat them. I was in love with Drake, would probably always be in love with him, but my heart and brain were still arguing about where I stood. So instead of saying another word, I pulled his head down and kissed him until neither one of us could think about anything except getting to bed.

--

Drake was still asleep when I left the next morning. The apartment was so quiet that I knew Shane was either out for a run or hadn't come home the night before. I hoped it was the former. If he was going to fuck anything with a vagina while he was pursuing my best friend, then I wasn't going to stand for that.

It was Saturday and I had a full to-do list screaming my name: laundry, homework, and dance practice with Linc. Somewhere in there I had to make time for a few extra special things before I saw Drake again tonight. As soon as I walked through my apartment door, I headed for the shower.

I should probably start leaving some of my things at Drake's, but I was trying to go slow with big things like that. I didn't want him to think that I was moving in and scare him. He hadn't even mentioned it, and I was okay with that. Really…

Harper was still sleeping soundly when I came out of our bathroom in nothing but a towel. My toothbrush was sticking out of my mouth as I pulled fresh underwear out of my bra and panty drawer. I was multitasking and making good time when Linc scared the hell out of me by walking in without knocking.

"Did you hear?"

I could only raise a brow at him because my mouth was full of toothpaste and spit. He grimaced. "The competition has been postponed because two of the judges got food poisoning last night. So we have three more weeks to practice."

I gave him a thumbs-up and walked back into the bathroom to rinse my mouth. "That's good news. I still haven't got that last swing perfect yet."

"Sorry, sweetheart, but I can't make it. I have a body builder's competition that weekend in Miami." He dropped down on my bed with a sigh. "Can you find someone else?"

I flopped down beside of him. "It's too late now. But don't worry about it." It was a little disappointing that I had worked so hard and wouldn't be able to compete, but it wasn't the end of the world for me. Besides, Linc and his drill sergeant routine had started to make the whole dancing thing less fun for me. "So, does that mean we don't have to practice this morning?"

"Not much use in it now."

"Great." I jumped up and started pulling on my clothes. "That means I have more time for other things…Want to go out with me this afternoon? Or do you have to work?"

"I don't have to go in unless they call me." Linc grinned and I had to stop looking at him for a moment. Damn that man was hot when he smiled like that. "So I'm all yours if you want me."

A pillow was suddenly tossed at my head, and I turned to find Harper glaring at me from her bed. "Keep it down. Sleeping here."

I blew her a kiss. "Sorry. I'm going." I grabbed my watch, phone, and shoulder bag before leaving. "Meet me later!" I said over my shoulder as I closed the door behind me and Linc.

"Much later!" Harper called back. She definitely wasn't a morning person. On days when she didn't have to be in work, she slept until after one. It was really crazy that she was the complete opposite of Shane. He was a morning person and could actually function on just a few hours of sleep. Harper, not so much! Shane was a man-whore and had fucked more women than I would ever care to count. Harper was still holding onto her V-card.

Dallas was just coming through the door as I reached the living room. She had an unkempt look to her, but that could mean just about anything when it came to her. Late night party? Maybe. Early morning breakfast with her mother and she had wanted to go for the grunge look to piss the woman off? It wouldn't be the first time it had happened.

All night love fest with the rock god?

Perhaps.

"I don't want to talk about it," Dallas muttered as she brushed passed me to get to her room.

"Noted." I grinned. "I'll just ask Ax." She shot me a glare but didn't say anything as she continued on down the hall. "Two thirty!"

"Yeah. I know. See you then," she grumbled as the door to her room slammed shut behind her.

Linc shook his head as he pushed the call button for the elevator. "She so has that 'I've been fucked to within an inch of my life' look going on. Cage must be really good in the sac."

I laughed. "I wouldn't know."

He rolled his eyes at me. "No. But that's only because you have another rock star to rub up against at night...And just when am I going to get to meet this one? I've already meet the brother-in-law and the future brother-in-law. When am I going to meet the brother that goes with them?"

Linc insinuating that Shane was my future in-law made my heart stutter. I hadn't let myself think along those lines for me and Drake. It had only been a little over a month since we had started seeing each other. Sure he had said he loved me the night before, but that didn't mean he was going to put a ring on my finger.

"Seriously, Lana. When am I going to meet Drake?"

I sighed. "Soon."

In all honesty, I was avoiding introducing my friend to my boyfriend. When Jesse and Shane had met Linc they had both gone all territorial alpha until I convinced them that Linc really was gay. So I could only imagine what Drake's reaction would be when he came face to face with the man I had been spending so much time with.

But it wasn't being fair to Linc to keep him out of the picture. It wasn't like he was some secret that I wanted to keep hidden away. I loved the guy like a brother. "I'll arrange a dinner for us all to meet. Maybe I will even invite Axton just to fuck with Dallas."

Linc laughed. "Sounds perfect to me."

THE ROCKER THAT NEEDS ME

Chapter 19
Drake

I frowned down at my phone for what felt like the millionth time.

It was just after six and I had finally gotten a break from listening to wannabe rockers. I was actually surprised today because I had actually liked a few of the hopefuls, and even said yes to a few that I had been only half sure of. I was in a good mood today, especially after the day and night before.

But Lana hadn't called or texted me all day. She wasn't answering when I called and my five texts had already gone unanswered. That never happened with my angel. She couldn't stand to not look at her cell when it chimed. So she either didn't have it with her...or she was avoiding me.

My stomach knotted up as the night before played in my mind. I had confessed my love to her, but she hadn't returned the words. At the time, I had been okay with that. Fuck, it had only been five weeks. She was probably still learning to trust me. But with each passing minute, each unanswered message I left, I started to second guess it all.

Maybe the incredible night we had shared the night before was her way of letting me down easily? She didn't love me after all...

"Dude, you okay?" Axton asked beside me. The producers were letting us out earlier than normal tonight, and tomorrow we actually had the day off. It was a welcome reprieve after nearly two months of long hours and no time off. I was pretty sure that Emmie had something to do with it after the last time I had complained to her, but it could also be because the producers were getting close to the number of hopefuls that they wanted for the show.

I shrugged. "Lana's not picking up her phone."

"Maybe it's dead." He was punching in something on his phone and seconds later it chimed with an incoming text. "Dallas says that she's with her, that Lana is okay, but unable to answer her phone right now."

I jerked the phone from my friend's hands and stared down at the screen. Seconds later, I typed in a message asking Dallas if Lana was coming over tonight. In the last month we hadn't spent one night apart. It chimed and I felt my heart move to my throat. "She's too busy to come over," I read aloud.

So it was true. Lana was avoiding me. What was I going to do if she broke up with me? But even as the thought left my mind, my emotions switched gears and the hurt and grief were pushed to the back as anger tried to consume me. She was too young, something I had known all along. Our relationship was too much for a little girl like her. Proof of which was her childishness in avoiding the issue instead of facing it full on.

The need for a drink nearly consumed me, and I pulled out my own phone once more to call Shane. He picked up after five rings. "Hey." He sounded distracted.

"I..." The sound of several females laughing in the background alerted me to the fact that my brother was probably off doing only God knew what. He had been really good the last few weeks so I decided to let him have his fun. "Never mind. See you later."

"Okay. See ya, bro." And he hung up.

"Want to grab some dinner?" Axton asked from my left. "I'm starving."

I shook my head, still lost in my emotions and the overwhelming need for a bottle of Jack. "I think I'm going to just head home." To an empty apartment, to lie on a bed that would smell like Lana, to memories that would drive me up the wall because I was sure that she was giving me the boot.

Axton gave me a strange look. "Are you okay? Want to come over to my place? Liam is in town and staying with me."

165

The thought of seeing Liam Bryant, lead bassist of OtherWorld, actually distracted me from some of the hurricane force emotions raging inside of me. I hadn't seen my friend in months, maybe as long as a year. The man was a crazy bastard that liked to live hard and partied harder.

Which was why I wasn't surprised when the penthouse was full of people when Axton and I arrived a while later. It was only after seven but the party was in full swing and I doubted that there was an end in sight. Axton took a look around his living room, taking in the girls on the sofa practically having sex with some guy that looked high as fuck. Across the room a group of people were playing strip beer pong. Music was blaring so loud that the walls vibrated and the booze was flowing like water.

The urge for a drink, which had been hitting me hard all evening, punched me in the gut. I knew that if I didn't leave right now I wasn't going to be able to fight the temptation for long. Axton shot me an apologetic grimace. "Sorry. I had no idea he was going to pull this shit."

"It's okay." But I wasn't so sure if it was. My gaze kept going to the bottles of whiskey just a few feet away.

"Let me find Liam and tell him to get these people the fuck out of my house and we can go grab something to eat." He turned and disappeared into the crowd of partiers.

I stood there, nearly frozen in my attempt to keep my feet from carrying me toward the bottles of liquor. That voice, the one that was my need for the alcohol, screamed that we needed to grab a bottle and start chugging. The one that normally said that I couldn't was so quiet I couldn't even hear it over the noise of the party…

Someone bumped into me and I turned my head to find Gabriella Moreitti standing next to me, looking just a little unsteady on her feet. I reached out to keep her from falling over and she fell against my chest. "It's a Demon," she murmured. "Oh, good, it's the fun one… No wait. It's the drunk one." She sighed. "I was hoping it would be the fun one. I really need to get laid!"

I wasn't sure if she was talking to me or herself. "I don't think my brother would take you up on the offer," I told her, stepping back and releasing her once I knew she wasn't going to fall over. "He knows that Emmie would cut off his balls."

Gabriella grimaced. "Ah, yes, the sainted Emmie." She rolled her eyes. "Don't want to upset her." Laughing, she stumbled away.

I watched her go then looked around for Axton, but there was no sign of my friend. Muttering a curse, I pulled out my phone and punched in Lana's number. It went straight to voicemail, and I threw my phone across the room. It bounced a few times then disappeared into the crowd.

Two more minutes and still no Axton. The smart thing to do would be just to leave, get myself out of the way of temptation...

Lana

I didn't get home until late. After the afternoon spent with all my friends as they watched my back turn into a work of art, we had all decided to grab a late dinner and then we split up. Dallas and Linc had gone clubbing, a typical Saturday night for those two. As much as they bickered and picked at each other, Linc and Dallas loved each other, and Linc couldn't relax at the club unless Dallas was with him. I wasn't sure, because I hadn't ever gone with them, but I thought that maybe Dallas helped Linc find suitable guys.

Harper and Shane went to a late movie. It had been sweet watching those two all afternoon and evening. My worry that Shane was only playing around with my best friend was put at ease for the most part since I could see the way he looked at her when he thought no one was watching. He didn't ogle her, didn't try to disrespect her by undressing her with his eyes whenever her back was turned. The biggest pass I had seen

167

him make toward her all evening was trying to hold her hand as we had walked to dinner from The Ink Shop.

I was home alone and really kind of exhausted on top of having some bad PMS cramps. It took a lot out of a person to have your back inked to the degree mine had been inked today. But it was well worth it. I was thrilled with the results. In the bathroom, I pulled off my top and tried to angle my back to get another peek, but it was bandaged. With a happy sigh, I left my shirt off, finished stripping and went back into my room that I shared with Harper and lay down on my stomach, hoping that the cramps would go away soon.

Within seconds I was asleep...

Hours later I turned over, reaching for Drake to snuggle up to. When I didn't feel him my eyes snapped open and I saw that I was at home instead of at his apartment. My stomach tensed up and I reached for my phone. I should have told him what I was doing. I should have told him myself that I wasn't going to get to see him yesterday evening.

I had wanted him to see my tattoo right away, hoping that it would tell him what I couldn't say out loud yet. Instead, I had let Shane talk me into letting the ink set over night before letting Drake see the masterpiece on my back.

Heart racing, I pulled up his name and hit connect. When it did nothing but ring until it went to voicemail, I glanced at the clock between my bed and Harper's. Two o'clock. Biting my lip I hit redial and was sent to his mailbox again. Three more times—nothing. That wasn't like Drake. He wasn't the heaviest sleeper. My repeated calls should have woken him up.

Without giving it much thought, I turned on the lamp and then remembered Harper, but she wasn't even in her bed. Not wanting to go down that road, wondering if my best friend was out getting nasty with the man I wanted as my brother-in-law, I started pulling on clothes. I had to get to Drake and tell him why I hadn't called. I missed him like an amputated limb, and my chest was already feeling like there was an elephant sitting on top of it.

The air was muggy as I hailed a taxi. I climbed in and gave the driver Drake's address. The city was calmer this time of night, and the man didn't have any trouble getting me there quickly. Still, I couldn't help feeling anxious. When the yellow car pulled to a stop in front of Drake's building, I tossed the guy a few bills, not caring that I had just tipped him out the ass, and rushed inside.

The doorman behind the desk gave me a welcoming smile when he saw me. "Morning, Miss Daniels."

I gave him a small smile. "Hey, Kyle," I greeted the hulking man. The security here was amazing, something I was sure that Emmie had made sure of before buying the apartment for Drake and Shane. But even if it hadn't been, the muscled man that stood guard over the lobby on the nightshift would have made intruders think twice before attempting anything.

The elevator came quickly when I called for it, and I waved at the doorman before stepping inside. The closer I got to his floor, the more nervous I got. My palms were sweating and my heart was racing. Dammit, it had been less than a day since I had left him sleeping in what I had come to think of as our bed, but I felt as if I hadn't seen him in months.

Using my key, I unlocked the apartment door...

Shane was standing in the living room. He jerked around as soon as he heard the door opening. I raised a brow at him. "I thought you would be with Harper." Worry for my friend suddenly made me freeze. Harper hadn't been at home!

"She's here," he assured me. "In the bedroom..."

"Shane!"

"No. Nothing happened." But I could see from his eyes that something *had* happened...

But what?

169

"Don't play games with her, Shane," I told him as I tossed my keys on the coffee table. "She's not like your usual women."

"I know that, sis..." His gaze kept moving down the hall and I watched as his jaw clenched so hard that I wondered if his teeth were going to break. "You should go," he said without turning his eyes away from the hall that led to the bedroom.

Drake's bedroom.

"I just got here. I missed Drake." I started toward the hallway that led to his room. "I'm tired, Shane. I'll see you in the morning."

"No!" He moved so fast my head spun. Shane stepped in my path and grasped my arms. "I think you should just go home. I'll make him call you. You guys can talk then."

"What is your problem?" I pulled my arms free and pushed against him to get him out of my way. "I'm not up for games, Shane. Really, I love you, but I'm tired. My back aches and I just want to snuggle up to Drake." He wouldn't move out of my way. I pushed at his chest, but he was unmovable.

"I'm telling you, Lana." His eyes were dark, a mixture of emotions swirling in his blue-gray eyes. "Go home."

My stomach tensed as I saw rage, disappointment, and worry among the emotions in Shane's eyes. I stopped trying to get around him. "Is Drake alright?" I demanded.

Shane grimaced. "That's a matter of opinion. Right now he's sleeping. In the morning, I plan to kill him." He reached out and his fingers gently pushed my hair away from my face. "Don't hurt yourself by going in there."

The first crack started at the bottom. I felt the pain in my heart but it wasn't enough to make me fall on my knees. "I need to see it." Whatever 'it' was. But with Drake that could be anything. "Please, Shane. Get out of my way."

He closed his eyes, as if mentally debating with himself over the decision to move or not. After a long moment he finally nodded and stepped to the side. My fingers shook as I reached for the doorknob, I could feel Shane standing just behind me, and I sucked in a steadying breath as I opened the door.

Nothing could have prepared me for what I saw when I stepped into that bedroom. The smell hit me first. Sweat and liquor mixed with some expensive perfume. My eyes zeroed in on the bed. Drake was asleep on top of the covers, completely naked. He was turned on his side, his pillow under him...

And a naked Gabriella Moreitti with her ass snuggled up to Drake's crotch. The crack in my heart tore upward, but I was numb. I felt like I was having an out of body experience, like I was watching everything happen from a distance. My body felt cold, my eyes oddly dry. There was no rage, like I was sure there should have been. No murderous craving for vengeance. Without realizing it, I moved to the side of the bed where Drake was.

He groaned when I leaned over and kissed is cheek. "Goodbye, Drake," I whispered.

As I straightened, he stretched out and turned on his back. Even as I turned away his eyes opened. "Is it morning yet?" he asked, a slur to his words even now. "Come back to bed, Angel."

I didn't turn around as I moved toward the door and met Shane. His face was clouded with emotions, but I saw the tears glazing those beautiful eyes of his. I knew that he was hurting for me. As I went to move past him he pulled me into his arms and kissed my forehead. "I'm sorry," he whispered.

I didn't raise my head to meet his eyes. "You have nothing to be sorry for," I assured him and stepped back. "I...I'll see you around, Shane."

"Angel?" Drake was waking up more now. I closed my eyes, trying to draw strength from deep down as I finally turned and met his gaze.

"Bye, Drake," I said in a dead voice and walked away.

171

Chapter 20
...Emmie...

I wasn't completely asleep when my phone rang.

Nik was playing with my hair, his fingers stroking through the ends in a way that was both soothing and arousing. It wasn't too late, just after eleven, but I had learned that with a baby eleven was late enough.

Nik's dick was twitching every now and then against my ass. I wasn't sure if he was just teasing me, or if he was going to try to get me to turn over and let him prove all over again that he worshiped my body. I was also unsure as to whether or not I would let him. Mia would be up at the crack of dawn wanting a dry diaper and some breakfast.

But still, this was Nik. He was worth feeling sleep deprived.

That thought was just crossing my mind when my phone went off. Nik sighed and kissed my cheek as he reached across me and picked up the phone from my bedside table.

"It's Shane," he informed me with a frown.

"Answer it," I told him, still clinging to that pre-sleep phase.

"Hello?" Nik paused and I could feel the tension filling his body.

That tension was all I needed to wake up. Something told me I wasn't going to like the reason for Shane's call. It was after two on the East Coast, so I was sure that whatever was going on wasn't going to be amusing. He knew better than to call after nine my time because of Mia's bedtime. The look on Nik's face confirmed my suspicions. His blue eyes were on fire with a temper that looked close to boiling over.

Nik kept listening for a long moment and then, without another word, he gave me the phone. Muttering some curses that I would have smacked him in the back of the head for saying in front of our daughter or Lucy, he started pulling on clothes.

"Shane?" I greeted.

"Emmie!" Shane sounded strange to me. A mixture of emotions in the way he said my name. My heart clenched because whatever was wrong was bad. Very bad. "Emmie, I need you."

"What's going on? Are you okay? Is Drake?" Fear made me grip the phone tighter. "Lana?"

"I... Drake got drunk at a party at Axton's. Liam is in town and he threw a party without Axton knowing about it. Axton invited Drake over after work yesterday and... He started drinking again, Em."

I bit my lip. "That isn't the end of the world, Shane. We all knew that he could have set backs. All we have to do is show him that we love him and support him through..."

Shane cut me off. "Emmie, that isn't what I'm calling you about!" He paused, blowing out a frustrated sigh. "Drake is passed out in his bed, Emmie. And he isn't alone."

"Don't tell me he got Lana drunk too!" I pushed the hair out of my face, already imagining the fit that Jesse was going to throw as soon as he heard about Lana's partying with Drake...

"It isn't Lana." The words came out soft, as if he was trying to break something major to me. I wasn't all that worried about myself right then. Drake had cheated on Lana. Oh, fuck! Jesse was going to kill him!

"Gabriella Moreitti is in bed with him."

My head snapped back as if Shane had physically slapped me. No. No. NO! "I don't believe you," I whispered. I thought I was rid of that stupid bitch when Axton told me he had called things off with her. He hadn't reverted to his old ways and let her back in his life after the last bitchy trick she had pulled months ago. Now...

"I swear to you, Emmie. I witnessed it with my own eyes. They are both naked and in bed...Lana just left..."

173

"Lana! Why the fuck wasn't she with him in the first place?" I demanded.

"Because she was with me all afternoon yesterday getting ink. She wanted to surprise him with... That doesn't even matter right now, Emmie!" he exclaimed. "Don't you dare put this off on Lana. She's destroyed right now!"

I sucked in a deep breath, trying to gain control over myself. I couldn't keep blaming Lana for Drake's mistakes. Everything she had ever done had been to help him, even if I hadn't seen it that way at the time. Lana was the best thing to ever happen to Drake.

And now he had completely fucked that all up!

Not even I could fix this for him.

"He's still passed out, Emmie. Both of them are."

"What do you want me to do, Shane?" I asked.

He blew out a long breath full of frustration, disgust, disappointment, and rage. "If you can't come take care of this, then no one will. Because if I have to do it, I will kill him. Lana is... I think she needs Layla."

"How pissed was she?" I know I would have been tearing the place apart if I had found Nik in the same situation. And Lana, she was as big a firecracker as I was when it came to raging.

"That's just it. She was all calm. Her eyes were all dead, and she even kissed him goodbye before leaving. She wasn't herself. I'm worried about her. Please, Emmie. Come help me." His voice was broken.

"I'll be on the next flight out."

"Thank you, Emmie."

"I have to go. I love you."

"Love you, Em!" And he hung up.

Nik was already tossing my clothes into a carry-on. "What can I do?" he asked from across the bedroom at my closet.

"I have to go to New York."

"I know. Should I stay here with Mia? Or do you think we should take her?" He looked concerned.

I bit my lip again. I hadn't spent one night away from my baby girl since we had brought her home from the hospital. "I don't know."

Nik stopped what he was doing and came back to me. "Get Jesse, Layla, and yourself on tonight's flight. If this takes more than a few days, then I will bring Mia and Lucy out. Okay?"

I nodded, tears already spilling from my eyes. Nik kissed me tenderly and pushed my phone into my hands. "It's going to be okay, baby. Mia will be okay."

"I know..." Closing my eyes, I sucked in a deep breath. After a moment, I opened my eyes and hit Jesse's name on my contact list.

It rang and rang and rang. When it went to voice mail, I hung up and dialed it again. "This better be good," Jesse growled into the receiver several rings later.

"Jesse."

"Emmie?" He was awake now and I was sorry that I had scared him. "Are you okay?"

"I'm fine," I assured him. "But you need to wake Layla up. Pack her a bag and I'll pick you both up. Drake..." How did I tell him without him going nuts? How did I keep one of the guys I loved so much from killing another one of the important men in my life?

"What about Drake?" he demanded. "Is he okay?"

"He's fine." For now, I thought as I pulled on a pair of jeans. "Listen, I will explain on the way to the airport. Just get ready."

"Okay. Okay." He sounded stressed. "It isn't Lana, is it?" His voice cracked and I closed my eyes. Layla and her sisters were his world now. If anything happened to any one of them it would destroy him. Which was why I feared for Drake's life!

"Lana is fine. She and Drake are having some issues. That's why I need Layla. Okay? Now hurry, Jesse!" I hung up before he could question me further. "Nik, will you call a taxi?" I asked even as I was surfing my phone for LAX.

It took twenty minutes and paying double what I would normally have agreed to pay, but I got the three of us on a flight for one o'clock out of LAX into JFK. As soon as the taxi pulled up, I hauled ass. I kissed Nik goodbye, fighting tears as I had to leave him and Mia behind even for a day or two. Jesse and Layla were already outside waiting for me. Nik was going to walk over and pick Lucy up.

Layla looked wild as she climbed in the back seat beside me. My best friend hugged me tight. "Is she okay? Really?"

"There are different types of *okay*, Layla," I told her. "I'm just not sure which type she falls into."

Jesse's eyes darkened. As the taxi driver drove like the hounds of Hell were after him, which was what I was paying him good money to do, I could see the way his eyes changed colors with his emotions.

"What happened?" he demanded, and I knew that he wasn't going to take my evasion tactics any longer.

So I told them what I knew. They were quiet, their tempers growing as they listened to me, and I was just finishing up by the time the taxi pulled to a stop in front of LAX. We had exactly fifteen minutes to get our tickets, get through security, and board our plane, but I had so much experience with cutting it close like this that it went smoothly.

With just two minutes to spare, we dropped into our seats. Unfortunately, none of us were seated together. I was smashed between two business men while Jesse was in the very back of the plane with three older ladies who were on their way to visit their grandchildren. Layla had it the easiest. She had a window seat with two teenaged girls beside of her that were already asleep by the time the plane took off.

Five and a half hours later, the plane touched down. It was almost seven, and I wasn't in any mood to be trifled with as I pushed us all into a cab and barked out the address for Drake and Shane's apartment. I knew that Lana needed us, but Drake had to be taken care of first.

Drake *and* Gabriella.

If that little slut was still there when I arrived, I was going to do what I should have done the first time she gave me that twisted, bitchy smile. Her classic, Italian beauty wasn't going to be very pretty when I got done with her!

Drake

Cotton mouth woke me from a dead sleep.

Groaning, I reached for Lana, wanting to kiss her before I got up for a glass of water. When I didn't feel her, my eyes snapped open and my head felt like it was going to split in two, but that didn't matter right then. Lana's side of the bed was rumpled and still felt warm, but she was gone. The sound of the shower calmed my racing heart and the sudden fear that she wasn't there.

I closed my eyes again, trying to take stock of my aches and pains. I was hung over, that much was obvious to me. Besides a pounding head, cotton mouth, and a queasy stomach, I was okay. I was mad as hell at myself for backtracking and swore that I wasn't going to let that happen again.

The shower turned off in the bathroom and I sighed, ready to face Lana's wrath. I deserved for her to be pissed, but I knew that she would forgive me for this slip. Even if she hadn't said the words Friday, I knew that she loved me...

The bathroom door opened. I jumped out of bed so fast I nearly fell on my face. My head and stomach protested, but I didn't give a fuck if I threw up or passed out. "What the fuck are you doing here?"

Gabriella grimaced at my loud voice. "Dude, down an octave please. Some of us aren't used to a raging hangover like the pro that you are." She held her towel around her with one hand and touched her temple with the other.

My mind, still cloudy with the after effects of liquor, was going crazy. The day before flashed through my brain: being upset over not seeing or talking to Lana all day, going to Axton's to visit with Liam, the party, Gabriella stumbling around, the urge to drink, and the overpowering need to down a bottle!

My fingers started shaking and I ran them through my hair. I hadn't been able to resist the need and had grabbed the first bottle I saw. Of course it had been Jack Daniels. I had downed the nearly full bottle in a matter of minutes. By the time Axton had come back to find me, I was out of it because it had been so long since my last drink...

From there everything was a solid blank—no fuzzy memories, nothing, just a big black void. That shouldn't have surprised me. Downing a bottle that fast always made me black out, but that didn't mean I hadn't done something stupid.

Like take home the one woman that would get my head knocked off by Emmie.

Oh, fuck that! What was I going to do about Lana?

"Did we..?" I couldn't bring myself to say the words *"have sex."* That would just be the nail in my coffin. That would mean the end of everything I loved and cherished. Oh, GOD! I had fucked up so bad.

"No." Gabriella shook her dark head. "No sex."

"Fuck!" I felt the tears sting my sinus cavity. That didn't mean shit! So what if I hadn't had sex with her? She had still been in my room and I had been drunk. Something must have happened even if we didn't have sex. "Get your fucking clothes on and get out!" I bellowed.

"Trust me, Demon. I was doing just that. I'm not exactly proud of myself, you know." She dropped her towel and pulled on her panties. The sight of her naked body did nothing for me. If anything, I was more disgusted—disgusted with her, but mostly myself.

178

I put on a pair of boxers and followed her out of my room to make sure that she left. I felt the tension as soon as I left the bedroom, knew that I was about to walk into a war zone the second I opened the door. Clenching my jaw I took a step forward, ready to face this like a man...

Man or not, I wasn't ready for the punch that Layla aimed at my throat!

She was standing by the couch, blocking Gabriella's path to the door. She was glaring at Gabriella hard, her body tense, ready to pounce. I was debating on whether to step in or not, leaning more toward not, when suddenly I couldn't draw a breath.

A wheeze escaped me and I doubled over, trying to suck in air. The fact that I had nearly swallowed my Adam's apple wasn't lost on me as I fought through the pain.

"Do you think I would just let you walk past me without dealing with you?" I heard Layla saying. Her tone was so frosty, goose bumps popped up on my arms. "I don't let little bitches like you hurt my family."

Gabriella screamed in pain and I raised my head to find her on the couch where Layla had pushed her over. The little Italian was probably second guessing her choice of keeping her hair long as Layla wrapped it around her fist and shook Gabriella's head like a rag doll while she screamed in her face.

"I will fucking end you!" Layla spit in her face. "Do you hear me, bitch? End you!"

Jesse pulled his wife off the other woman. "Okay, babe. I think she gets the point." With his arms wrapped tightly around Layla's waist, he pulled her back, but she was still kicking and swinging her arms in her determination to do just as she had promised.

Gabriella had a bleeding lip, and I saw a hand full of hair still gripped in Layla's hand. Tears poured down Gabriella's face. "I didn't screw the Demon!" she screamed back at Layla once Jesse had her at a safe distance. "We didn't even kiss."

"Yeah, so that explains why you were naked in bed with him." Emmie's frosty voice came from across the living room, and I turned my head to see her sitting on the chair as if a cat fight hadn't just take place mere feet from her. Fuck, she was pissed. I could see the temper that went with that red hair of hers burning in those wild green eyes.

"I was drunk!" Gabriella excused. "I didn't think about it when I was trying to get comfortable."

One brow rose. "Why were you even here in the first place?"

"He could barely stand after the second bottle. Axton was off with his new flavor of the month trying to keep Liam from screwing with her. I felt bad for the drunken slob." Gabriella wiped her bleeding lip with the hem of her shirt. "So I helped him home. Even as drunk as I was, I still wasn't nearly as gone as he was."

Emmie sat there staring at Gabriella for a full minute. Her eyes narrowed at the other woman, as if looking for any signs that she was lying. God, I hoped she wasn't lying because I didn't know what I was going to do if something *had* happened.

"Get out, Gabriella. Don't look at any of my guys again or you will think that the beating Layla just gave you was a tickle compared to what I will do to you."

The pain was fading now, so I saw the look cross Gabriella's face. The bitch really didn't know when to stop when she was ahead. I grimaced as she opened her smart-ass mouth. "What are you going to do, little miss perfect? Nothing, that's what, or you would have done it when I told you that BS about your precious Nik..."

She broke off with a scream as Emmie went flying at her, nails pointed right for her pretty face. Gabriella tried to protect her face as Emmie's fists swung back. The sound of slapping echoed in the room, and I saw another handful of Gabriella's hair, gripped in Emmie's hands this time. Emmie's curses would have had a sailor blushing the way she spat them out.

"Emmie!" Jesse had given her a good two minutes before he tried to step in, but Emmie was too far gone in her rage. "Enough, Em!" He tried to pull her off the other woman but only got a scratch across his cheek to show for his efforts.

I wasn't about to step in. Gabriella deserved everything she was getting. If she had been smart, she would have kept her mouth shut and left. Instead, she had opened that mouth of hers, and Emmie had been unable to control herself a moment longer. It had been more than two years coming, but the dam was now busted wide open, and Emmie wasn't going to stop until she had it all out of her system.

It was Layla that put an end to the fighting. Still pissed at the other woman, she was none to gentle as she grabbed Gabriella by the hair and pulled her out from under Emmie. When Emmie went to follow, Layla put herself between the two of them. "She's had enough, Em." Layla's calm voice broke through Emmie's red haze. "She's just a little crying ball of fur now."

Layla pushed Gabriella away from her, and she landed on her ass—hard. Layla pulled Emmie into her arms, rocking her. "It's okay, Emmie."

Finally, Gabriella played it smart and left. I didn't give her a second glance as she brushed passed me. The door slammed shut behind her, but my gaze was on the two women sitting on my couch.

"You really need to cut your nails, Em," Jesse complained, and I got a good look at the scratch on his right cheek. It was about an inch long and bleeding.

"Fuck!" Emmie was full of remorse. "Oh, Jess, I'm sorry!"

"It's just a scratch, sweetheart." His gaze shifted to me. "In light of Gabriella's confession, I'm glad I don't have to stomp your fucking ass."

Chapter 21

Lana

My brain had shut down.

I left the apartment functioning on autopilot. I didn't remember the ride down in the elevator or Kyle the doorman speaking to me. I had no recollection of hailing the cab that drove me home or walking into my apartment. The faint smell of smoke and booze and sex, that should have told me that at least one of my roommates had returned, was lost on me as I opened the door to my shared room and fell across my bed without bothering to shut the door.

For the longest time, I just lay there on my stomach, not feeling much of anything other than the slight discomfort coming from my back and the PMS cramps that didn't seem to want to let up. I didn't think about anything. I couldn't. My mind was trying to protect my heart and had shut down as a safety mechanism.

The sky slowly lightened outside my window, but still I didn't notice. Through the open doorway, I heard someone moving around the apartment. From the sound of the heavy footsteps, I could only assume it was Linc. The second pair of heavy footsteps told me he had brought someone home last night.

I blinked, realizing that I had been staring at the same spot for hours. My eyes were dry and hurt. My entire body was one big ache. I sighed and sat up. I think I liked the numbness better.

From the corner of my eye, I saw a shadow in the doorway and turned my head to find Shane standing there. He looked pale, but his eyes were clouded with a mixture of emotions I didn't want to think about. The man that I had dreamed of being my brother-in-law was giving me a concerned look.

"How are you?" he asked, his voice rough.

I shrugged. "I don't really know," I told him honestly. I was waiting for the anger to hit me, the rage and humiliation.

Mostly, I was wondering why I wasn't crying. The man who was supposed to be my soul-mate, who had whispered that he loved me over and over again as he moved inside of my body, had been in bed with another woman. So why wasn't I bawling my eyes out?

"Jesse and Layla are over there. They arrived with Emmie about an hour ago." He took a few steps into my shared room. Big hands thrust into jean pockets, and he let his head fall back on his shoulders as he frowned up at the ceiling. "I'm sorry, sis."

I flinched. "Please don't call me that," I whispered.

"I... Yeah, okay." We were both quiet for a minute. "Do you want me to go?"

I pushed my tangled hair out of my face before shaking my head. "No, Shane. You can stay."

He looked relieved and sat down on the bed beside of me. "Want something to eat? Linc is making breakfast."

"No. I'm not hungry. My stomach is a little upset." In fact, I was fighting the urge to throw up. Damn shock! I was going to be a mess when it finally faded.

There was a light tapping on the open bedroom door, and I turned to find Harper standing in our shared room. "Hey." Her voice was gentle, causing my chest to ache just a little more. "How are you?"

I shrugged. "I'm still not sure."

"Want me to help you with your bandages?" She closed our bedroom door, and I saw that she had a new tube of A&D ointment in her hand. "You probably want some of this on it."

I nodded. "Thanks."

Shane stood and Harper took his place, his hand grasping and squeezing hers for a moment before stepping away. I watched as something passed between them, but it was over and gone so quickly I couldn't say what it had been.

Shane gave me a grim smile. "I think I'm going to go grab a bacon sandwich or something."

When the door shut behind him, I pulled my shirt over my head and Harper started pulling at the tape that held the gauze over my tattooed back. I waited until the bandages were gone before speaking. "Are you in love with him?"

Harper, in the process of opening the new tube of A&D ointment, stopped what she was doing. Her brow furrowed, as if she was really thinking about the answer to my question. After a moment she sighed. "Maybe."

I just nodded and turned back around so she could rub the ointment across my ink. I flinched a few times as she touched the sensitive, slightly welted skin. The tattoo took up most of my back. It really should have been done in two sittings, but I had wanted it bad and paid extra to get it done in one. Now...now it was just a reminder of a huge mistake.

"I never should have gotten involved with him again," I whispered. "I knew that it would only end in heartache, and maybe that was why I was holding off on telling him I love him. He's a rocker, something I should have always kept reminding myself of."

"Ah, sweetie. I know you are hurting right now. But maybe...maybe he didn't do anything. It could just be a misunderstanding."

"Maybe..." I agreed, but without much enthusiasm. I had little hope for that possibility.

--

I didn't leave my room for another hour and a half. By then it was nearly lunch time, but I was still feeling sick. The lingering smells of bacon and other breakfast foods turning my stomach, and I was fighting the urge to vomit more and more with each passing minute.

With the skin on my back still sensitive, I decided against a bra and put on a baggy tee shirt that belonged to Linc. His sleepover friend, who I learned Linc had met at the party he and Dallas had ended up at instead of going clubbing the night before, was still lounging on our sofa when I walked into the living room. Shane and Harper were sitting beside him watching television. The three of them, mostly the two guys, took up almost the entire couch, so I flopped down on the floor between Shane and Harper's legs.

"Feeling better?" Harper asked, noticing my paleness.

I was breathing through my mouth to keep from gaging. "Not really. I might need a bucket actually."

"Linc!" Harper yelled.

"What?!" His voice came from down the hall, probably his bedroom.

"We need your hangover bucket!" she told him.

I grimaced. Linc had a hangover almost every Sunday morning, but instead of sleeping it off he worked through his sickness. Most of the time that meant carrying around what we had deemed "the hangover bucket," which he threw up in when he had to, and then he went on about his day. Dallas swore she could still smell the contents even after it was bleached Monday mornings. I hoped that wasn't the case today.

Linc appeared with the little white waste basket. As he offered it to me, he frowned. "Want me to kick his ass?"

I offered him a small smile. "Nah, but thanks for the offer."

He winked. "Anything for you, beautiful."

The phone by the door rang, and I felt my stomach churn because I knew in my heart who it was. I ached to see my sister, and in truth Jesse and Emmie too. But I knew that Drake would be with them. As Linc moved to answer the phone, my stomach heaved and I emptied my dinner from the night before into the hangover bucket.

Shane's hands were cool on my neck as he rubbed soothingly. A damp washcloth was put against my forehead by Harper, and I closed my eyes, fighting the next wave of sickness. When I thought I had control of it all, I raised my head.

"Shane, I don't want them to see me like this," I whispered.

He just nodded and lifted me into his arms. "I've got you, Lana," he murmured as he carried me down the hall to my room.

From the edge of my bed, I heard the front door open. Through the open bedroom door, I could hear the feminine voices of my sister and Emmie. There was a long pause between greetings as Jesse spoke to Linc and his guest. Well, fuck! I had forgotten about the new guy.

"Shane, please make sure no one kills anyone while I brush my teeth," I told him.

"I'll do my best," he promised and closed the door behind him.

Harper lingered. "Need any help?"

I shook my head. "No, but thanks. Can you help him? They all have territory issues."

"Yeah, I've noticed." She sighed. "Yell if you need me."

When the door shut behind her I stood and went into our shared bathroom. I scrubbed the taste of vomit out of my mouth and prayed that I wouldn't have to do it again anytime soon. My hair looked like shit, and I pulled it up into a sloppy ponytail. As soon as I opened the bedroom door, I heard the raised male voices.

Linc and Drake.

I groaned, knowing that Drake was about to lose it. I should have introduced those two long before now, dammit!

"No way!" Drake yelled. "You are not the roommate. She said you were gay..."

"Dude, I am." I reached the living room in time to see Linc point at the shirtless guy still sitting on the couch. "See? That's the guy you saw me hanging out with last night. Remember? We talked for like twenty minutes last night, man. Me, you, Dallas, and Axton? Ring any bells there, man?"

"Of course he doesn't remember," I answered for him. "If he was inhaling Jack Daniels like I suspect he was, then he would be lucky to remember his own name today."

"Angel..."

For the first time I let my eyes go to him. He was pale, his eyes bloodshot and glassy. I remembered all the signs of his hangovers. I wondered how long he had spent with his head in the toilet that morning and if Emmie had to help him shower.

"Don't," I told him. "Don't ever use that word again." It felt like poison now; him calling me *Angel* felt like a white hot dagger stabbing me in the heart.

"Lana." Layla's cool hands touched my arm, and I turned my head to meet my sister's gaze. "Baby, are you okay? You look a little green."

"I don't want to talk about it, Layla." More than anything I wanted her to just hold me, to rock me in her arms the way she had when I was a little girl. But I knew that I had to deal with Drake on my own. Already, I could feel the tears that had evaded me for hours stinging my sinuses.

"I wish I could take last night back." Drake's voice had my head snapping around in his direction once more. He took several steps toward me, but my glare stopped him. "I know I let you down, Angel..."

"I said *don't*."

He faltered for just a second before clenching his jaw. "Nothing happened," he informed me, sounding so sure.

"And you know this because you remember? You know that nothing happened?" I demanded, not believing him for a minute.

"No, I don't remember anything from last night, Angel." His shoulders drooped just a little. "But..."

"But nothing!" I pulled away from my sister and took a step in his direction. "If you don't remember, then how can you be so sure that nothing happened?"

187

"Because your sister beat it out of Gabriella," Jesse's deep voice informed me.

"I... What?" I demanded, turning to face my brother-in-law. "She did what?"

Jesse had a look of pride on his face and a half-grin tilting his lips. "Yeah, I know. It was so hot. Between her and Em, I think the bitch is bald in a few places."

I was sure if my world wasn't falling apart right at that moment I would have laughed. My spit fire sister kicking Gabriella Moreitti's ass? I would have paid money to see that! But I was in no mood to laugh. "She admitted that nothing happened and you believed her?"

Jesse shrugged. "She may have only been saying that to get Layla off of her. Not that it worked. I had to pull her off. Em, what was your take? Do you think she was lying?"

Emmie had been quietly standing by the door. Her gaze taking everything in, missing nothing. When her green eyes met mine, I saw that she really had believed the other woman.

"I doubt that anything happened. Drake hadn't had a drink in months. That much liquor in his system...he was probably useless below the waist."

My eyes closed as hope flowed through me, but it was short lived. One night away from Drake and our lives—our future together—was all washed down the drain. "It wouldn't be the first time that he was that drunk and was able to function," I whispered.

"What are you saying, Lana?" Layla asked, but I could hear in her voice that she knew what I was telling her. "You...?"

I didn't answer her as I forced my gaze to meet Drake's. "You can't remember anything, but until you do, I won't ever believe that you didn't have sex with her."

He swallowed hard. "I'll never remember, Lana."

"Yeah, I know. Just like you will never remember our night together." His head snapped back as if I had punched him.

"Our night together?" He sounded strangled.

I knew that telling him now would only hurt him, but the bitch in me just didn't care. I was hurting, and I wanted him to hurt just as much. I wanted him to hurt more! "The night before Jesse and Layla got married? The night you took my virginity? I'm sure that night is a blank hole in your mind. Probably why you don't know why I was so shattered the next night when I heard you fucking some slut against the hotel room door that separated our rooms."

"No!" He was in front of me in just a few steps, his grip on my arms so tight it was painful. "Tell me that it didn't happen!" he demanded.

"I can't." I jerked out of his hold. There was no need to slap his face, not when he was already beaten from my admission.

"Are you done, now?" Emmie asked, calm as always. "Do you maybe want to pull out his heart and stomp on it too?"

"I think she just did that," Shane muttered for the first time, joining in. "And he has no one to blame but himself, Em."

"She knew that it would destroy him." Emmie pointed at me, looking wild. "She knew that she had all the power here, and she used it against him! If she loved him the way everyone seems to think she does, she never would have done that."

Her words were like a slap to my face. I couldn't find the words to defend myself against her because part of me knew that she was right. I stared at the man that stood with his head hung, tears falling form his eyes, and knew that I had made this mess. This was all my fault...

"She used it to protect herself! Drake is a grown man, he makes his own mistakes. Stop putting his mess on her shoulders."

I didn't even hear Shane's words. His voice was just background noise to me as I fought the urge to vomit. I had made a mess of my life, and I had ruined the future I had wanted so badly with Drake. With a pain filled cry, I turned and ran down the hall toward my room.

Chapter 22

Drake

I didn't know what to expect as I left my apartment with my out of town guests. Emmie flagged down a taxi as soon as we were out on the street, and I was the last to slide into the back. Layla gave me a grim little smile as Emmie gave the driver the address from the front seat.

I tried to return her smile, but my face felt frozen.

The ride felt like it took an eternity, but it was over far too soon. I was torn between wanting to hurry and fix this and wanting to put it off in hopes that it would just fix itself. When we reached Lana's building, we had to wait downstairs until someone let us up because Emmie and Layla had never been there before.

Some muscle head guy answered the door, and I noticed a shirtless guy seated on the couch that I had to assume was Linc because he was checking me out as soon as we stepped inside the apartment.

"Who the hell is this?" Jesse demanded.

Muscle Head glanced at the guy on the couch. "He's with me."

Shane came from down the hall, and I wondered if he had been in Lana's room. "It's cool, Jess. Lana is safe."

"Random guys come in and out of this place regularly?" Jesse asked, his brow furrowed and his eyes stormy. He sounded like a protective father.

"Not as often as you would think." Linc tried to put him at ease.

"Linc would never let anyone hurt us." Harper appeared behind Shane, her hand touching his back before stepping around him. "There's isn't anything to worry about."

"I don't like it," Jesse grumbled but didn't comment further. How could he without sounding like a hypocrite after all the years we had put Emmie in the line of one night stands? Some of those girls were dangerous in their own right, but Emmie had been able to take care of them.

"Linc, I think I'm going to go, man..." Shirtless said, eyeing us all with apprehension now.

That caught me off guard. Muscle Head was Linc? I couldn't picture him as gay. He was too...Not! "No way! You are not the roommate. She said you were gay..."

"Dude, I am." He pointed at the shirtless guy still sitting on the couch. "See? That's the guy you saw me hanging out with last night. Remember? We talked for like twenty minutes last night, man. Me, you, Dallas, and Axton? Ring any bells there, man?"

"Of course he doesn't remember." Lana's voice had my head snapping around. She looked pale, sick. My heart constricted. I did this to her! "If he was inhaling Jack Daniels like I suspect he was, then he would be lucky to remember his own name today."

"Angel..." I took a step toward her.

"Don't." Her voice was cold. "Don't ever use that word again."

Layla moved closer to her sister. She said something but I could only focus on Lana. Her shirt was three times too big on her, her yoga pants something that I had seen a thousand times. Her hair was a mess even pulled back into a ponytail. There was sweat on her upper lip and across her forehead, and I wondered if she was feeling ill.

"I wish I could take last night back," I told her, taking a few more steps closer. Maybe if I could just hold her everything would be okay. Her glare stopped me. "I know I let you down, Angel..."

"I said *don't*."

The words came out as a whisper, but they felt like they were shouted inside my head. She didn't want me to call her *Angel*. It was understandable after everything I had put her

192

through during the last twenty-four hours. That didn't mean it didn't hurt any less. "Nothing happened."

"And you know this because you remember? You know that nothing happened?"

"No, I don't remember anything from last night, Angel. But..."

"But nothing! If you don't remember, then how can you be so sure that nothing happened?"

"Because your sister beat it out of Gabriella," Jesse's assured her.

"I... What? She did what?"

Jesse had a look of pride on his face and a half-grin tilting his lips. "Yeah, I know. It was so hot. Between her and Em, I think the bitch is bald in a few places."

"She admitted that nothing happened and you believed her?" I thought there might have been hope in her voice.

Jesse shrugged. "She may have only been saying that to get Layla off of her. Not that it worked. I had to pull her off. Em, what was your take? Do you think she was lying?"

"I doubt that anything happened. Drake hadn't had a drink in months. That much liquor in his system...he was probably useless below the waist."

I wasn't in the least embarrassed to have Emmie talk about the probability of my dick working or not. If anything, I was relieved that she thought that. Maybe it would help convince Lana...

Lana's eyes closed and I thought she was relieved, that everything was going to be alright now... Her next words made my head spin. "It wouldn't be the first time that he was that drunk and was able to function," she whispered.

"What are you saying, Lana?" Layla asked. "You...?"

Lana's gaze locked with mine. "You can't remember anything, but until you do, I won't ever believe that you didn't have sex with her."

193

I swallowed hard, knowing that she was telling me that unless I did remember, we were over. "I'll never remember, Lana."

"Yeah, I know. Just like you will never remember our night together."

I felt like someone had actually punched me in the gut. "Our night together?" My voice was weak.

"The night before Jesse and Layla got married? The night you took my virginity?" Her whisky eyes were on fire. "I'm sure that night is a blank hole in your mind. Probably why you don't know why I was so shattered the next night when I heard you fucking some slut against the hotel room door that separated our rooms."

"No!" I moved without even realizing I was doing so. I grasped her arms, holding on to her even though I knew that I wasn't going to be able to hold on to *us*. "Tell me that it didn't happen!"

"I can't." She jerked away from me.

A sob seemed to be trapped in my chest, tears spilled, but I didn't care. The last nail was being hammered into my coffin, and I didn't know how to stop it. I was defenseless to stop the pain that was starting to consume me.

Emmie and Shane's raised voices didn't even penetrate the darkness surrounding me. Lana ran away from me, and I knew that my world had official stopped. Cold, gentle fingers touched my arm, and I blinked my eyes to see through my tears. Layla stood beside of me, her face a mixture of emotions. "I know this is hard, but you have to go. Jesse is going to kill you, Drake."

I glanced at my friend, seeing the storm building with each passing second. "Let him," I told her. An end to the pain I was feeling would be welcomed...

--

I don't know how I ended up on the floor.

One minute I was standing in Lana's living room, feeling the worst pain of my life, the next I was out cold. Emmie was leaning over me, her hand firmly tapping me on the cheek as she yelled my name over and over again. "Drake!"

I blinked, unable to keep my eyes open for longer than a second or two before I had to close them again. "Fuck!" I exclaimed, raising a hand to touch my throbbing jaw. "What happened?"

A shadow appeared over me, and I squinted up at my brother. "Layla tried to warn you, bro. Jesse has a freaking badass right hook on him." The brief glance I got of Shane's face told me he wasn't feeling any empathy for me. "You've been out for about two minutes."

I groaned, turning on my side so I could try to get up. "Where's Lana?" I demanded.

"In her room. Probably throwing up again." I shot Shane a frown as I straightened. "She hasn't been in the best shape this morning. Finding her boyfriend asleep with another woman's naked ass against his crotch tends to turn a girl's stomach."

"Fuck," I muttered, running a shaking hand through my hair. "I need to talk to her."

"You need to go home." Emmie's cool voice told me, and I turned to look down at her. "Jesse is holding onto his temper by his fingernails. Layla pushed him down the hall so he wouldn't kill you."

"I'm not leaving until I talk to Lana," I told her, pushing past my brother and heading toward Lana's bedroom. Jesse's punch must have knocked some sense into me because I was seeing things more clearly now. If I didn't talk to her now, didn't see her now, then I was going to lose her forever.

The muscle head stood in my way when I reached the hall that led to the bedrooms. Linc was a hulking brute, even bigger than Jesse in size and muscle. "Leave her alone, man. I don't want to kick your ass."

He was bigger than me, outweighed me by at least twenty pounds of pure muscle, but I wasn't in the frame of mind to care. I had only one goal and that was to get to Lana, to plead and beg for one more chance. No one was going to keep me from her.

"Lana!" Harper's scream was full of fear. Linc didn't even hesitate; he just turned and ran down the hall. Everyone followed, and I pushed through the masses of family and roommates to get into Lana's room.

She was lying in the doorway that led into the connecting bathroom. Harper was leaning over Lana, trying to make her wake up. Layla was already there staring down at her sister in horror. I followed her gaze and my heart stopped when I saw that her yoga pants were covered in blood.

"Lana, wake up!" Harper pleaded, as she tapped her on the cheek. "Please, please, please, wakeup."

Shane was just behind me, and when he saw the blood on Lana's pants, the blood that was still almost gushing out of her and flooding the tan carpet under her, he made a gagging noise. Emmie pushed him toward the door, her phone already to her ear. "Get out, Shane. Go wait for the paramedics!"

I bent down beside of Lana. Her face was pale, the life seeming to drain out of her. I grasped her hand. It was so cold. "Angel..." I whispered but she didn't even flinch.

Linc pushed Harper out of the way and felt Lana's neck for a pulse. "It's very slow." He said, looking over at Emmie who was on the phone barking out orders. I could only guess she was talking to 9-1-1.

My heart was racing, fear gripping me so hard I almost couldn't breathe. I wanted to do something, anything, but I was useless. It felt like an eternity before the paramedics arrived, but it was only ten minutes. My heart stopped when Linc yelled that Lana had stopped breathing just as the paramedics came through the door. I was pushed out of the way so they could get to her.

Layla was talking to the EMT in charge, asking if she could go with them, but they couldn't let her or anyone else, not when Lana was barely hanging on. As they loaded her onto the gurney, I reached for her hand once more. Her fingers were like ice now, and I was doing nothing but praying, almost willing her to live. I had heard what the paramedics had said, I knew what was wrong. One more thing I was responsible for. One more thing that threatened to take Lana away from me forever...

Lana was losing our baby.

Chapter 23
Lana

I sat on the end of my bed, my head in my hands as I sobbed. I had just destroyed the man I loved.

I knew that nothing happened the night before. I couldn't not believe it when both Layla and Emmie had beaten it out of Gabriella. It had just taken me a minute to get it straight in my head. Now I had to fix what I had broken in the next room, and I had no idea how I was going to do that.

I should never have told him about our night together. It hadn't done anything but hurt him, something that I had been aiming for as the words slipped from my mouth. But now I regretted it. Emmie was right. I did hold all the power and I had used it against Drake, when I should have loved him.

Harper knocked on our bedroom door, and I raised my head as she stuck hers around to look in at me. "Are you okay?"

I shrugged. "I don't know." That seemed to be my answer for everything today. "I messed up really bad, Harper."

She stepped into our room and closed the door behind her. "It will be okay, sweetie. Drake loves you just as much as you love him."

"I know." If nothing else, I knew that Drake loved me. He needed me, and I needed him. Sighing, I pushed the hair that had fallen from the ponytail out of my face. "Is he still here?"

"He's out cold right now. Your brother-in-law knocked his socks off." A grim smile twisted her mouth. "Layla has him in Linc's room trying to cool him down."

Perfect. Now, I had caused two men that had been friends all their lives to fight. "I better go deal with them then." I shifted on the edge of the bed and grimaced in pain. My cramps were getting worse. I sucked in a deep breath, trying to get through them without whimpering. My period was late, nothing unusual about that, but now that I was getting ready to start, it was going to be a real bitch to get through.

When the last one seemed to pass I got to my feet. "I just need a minute..." I murmured. As I took a step toward the bathroom the world seemed to tilt. I felt something thick and sticky run down my thighs and had enough sense to look down. My yoga pants were covered in blood...

The pain was awful. I had nothing else to compare it to. I blinked my eyes open, unsure what I was going to find. The hospital room wasn't on my list of things to expect to find. There were tubes coming from all directions: oxygen in my nose, an IV in my left arm, and a heart monitor on my chest. I shifted my legs and my entire body protested in pain. A whimper escaped me.

Strong, cold fingers brushed across my forehead. "Angel?"

"Drake?" I whispered his name. My lips were dry and cracked, my throat felt like I had swallowed glass. "What...happened?"

He was pale with a few days growth of hair on his jaw that hadn't been there when I last saw him. "I'm sorry, Angel. This is all my fault." His voice cracked and I saw the tears in his eyes.

I gripped his hand, scared. "Nothing is your fault. Stop thinking things like that." I tugged on his hand, pulling him closer. I had no idea what had happened, but I knew that Drake wasn't to blame for anything. "I love you, Drake."

The sob that left him made my heart ache. "I love you, Angel..." He kissed my forehead. "I love you more than anything in the world."

"What's wrong with me?" I asked. "Why do I hurt so bad?"

He closed his eyes. "You had a miscarriage. Our baby is gone."

If I thought I was in pain before, it was nothing compared to hearing those words. "I..." Tears blinded me. "I was pregnant?"

Drake nodded. "I'm sorry, Angel. I should have protected you."

"Stop saying you're sorry!" I cried. "You aren't the only one that is in this relationship, stupid. I knew we weren't being careful…" Maybe I had hoped for something to happen, like getting pregnant. I hadn't been worried about not being careful because deep down I had wanted Drake's baby. It was selfish, but I had secretly wanted that tie to him.

And I hadn't even known it had actually happened. Our child had been growing deep inside of me, and I hadn't known. A sob felt like it was being ripped from my chest. "Drake, our baby!"

He gathered me into his arms as much as he could without hurting me. "I know. I know, Angel," he whispered brokenly as he gently rocked me.

The door to my room opened so suddenly I was startled. A man with graying hair and a white coat came in with a nurse in pink scrubs right behind him. "Miss Daniels," he greeted, and I raised my head from Drake's chest. "It's good to see you awake."

I frowned at him. "How long have I been out?" Maybe that should have been my first question to Drake, but I was still a little disorientated and was finding it even harder to focus with the news that Drake had given me.

"Three days, off and on." The doctor put his iPad on the little table beside of my bed, and Drake reluctantly stepped back to give the doctor access to me. "You have had everyone in the waiting room on pins and needles waiting for you to wake up. Mr. Stevenson here has refused to leave your side, and your sister has been driving my staff up the wall wanting an hourly progress report…" a small smile tilted his lips "…but we have managed."

I couldn't find the will to return his smile. I hurt too badly, physically and emotionally. "Drake said I had a miscarriage."

The doctor nodded. "Yes… These things sometimes happen in first pregnancies, but yours was a little different. You had an ectopic pregnancy, where the baby settled in your fallopian tube, and as it grew that tube ruptured. You nearly bled to death. I had to remove the tube."

My hand went to my lower stomach, and I felt the bandage that covered the incision. "Will I…" I broke off and raised my eyes to meet Drake's "…will I be able to have another baby?"

"Because of the removal of the fallopian your chances of conceiving have been cut in half, but I see no reason for you not to be able to have another baby."

Relief washed over me and the tears started falling once more. "Really?"

The doctor nodded. "You are a healthy young woman. There is no reason that you shouldn't."

It took the doctor ten minutes to examine me. I was one big ache by the time he and his nurse left with a promise of bringing me pain medication soon. I lay back against the pillows while Drake continued to look out the window where he had been the whole time the doctor was checking me over. "Drake?"

His shoulders lifted and fell as he let out a long breath, but he didn't turn around. "I do nothing but hurt you."

I closed my eyes, scared that he was about to tell me goodbye. "No."

"Yes." His movements were jerky as he finally turned around to face me. "I took advantage of you back in December then cheated on you the next day." I flinched at the remembered pain that had caused. "Then I turn around and do the same thing. I'm all kinds of wrong for you, Lana."

"Angel," I whispered, and he frowned.

"What?"

A tear spilled down my cheek, and I quickly brushed it away. "Angel. Not Lana, never Lana again. I'm your angel, Drake. Don't ever call me Lana again."

"I..."

"And you are wrong. I don't think you cheated with Gabriella. Even drunk, you wouldn't do that, especially with her." I lifted my hand, offering it to him, silently begging him to come to me. "You aren't wrong for me, Drake. You're the best thing in my world. I can't imagine my life without you."

He took a hesitating step forward. "I love you, Angel. More than anything, I love you."

"I love you too." It came out a vow, which it was. "Hold me, Drake. Please hold me."

He moved quickly and then his arms were around me, and I felt some of my tension ease. "I thought I had lost you." His tears soaked my neck as he buried his face in my shoulder. "I thought I had lost my reason for living."

I combed my fingers through his hair, soothing us both a little. "You could never lose me, babe. I'm yours, forever."

--

I was almost asleep when I heard the door to my private room open. Thinking it was Drake coming back after visiting hours, even though I had made him promise to go home and sleep, I raised my head. If I were honest, I would admit to being selfish enough to want Drake to come back, even though I knew he was dead on his feet after sitting beside my bed for the last three days.

It wasn't Drake, however. I blinked in the dim lighting coming from the tall street lamps outside my window, thinking at first that I was indeed asleep and dreamed the man that quietly made his way toward me. I was awake, and he was very real.

"What are you doing here, Cole?" I demanded, my voice hoarse from the tube that had been down my throat during my emergency surgery three days before.

He stopped a few feet away. I couldn't see his eyes in the dim light, but his face appeared pale. "Axton and I came to visit you yesterday, and I spoke to your sister and brother-in-law." His voice was gruff, full of some emotion I couldn't place in the old rocker. "Why didn't you tell me, Lana?"

My heart turned cold, and I pulled the covers up to my chest. "Tell you what?" I tried to play dumb, but he wasn't having any of that.

"You are my daughter." He thrust his hands into his jean pockets as he frowned down at me. I wished I could see his eyes, those eyes that were identical to my own, but they were in the shadows. "Would you have ever told me yourself?"

I clenched my jaw, upset with my sister and Jesse for telling this man anything. "Probably not," I told him truthfully.

A small grin tilted his lips even though his brow was still furrowed. "At least you're honest. You have fire, Lana. God, you remind me..."

"If you say I remind you of you, I will throw something at your head!"

"...my sister," he finished, a full blown grin making his face relax in a way that made him look at least ten years younger. "You remind me of my sister. You look a little like her, actually. I'm surprised that I didn't notice it before."

I didn't want to get into a big discussion with Cole Steel. "What do you want, Cole?"

The grin disappeared. "I wanted to see how you are doing. To make sure that you were okay."

I felt anger start to boil in my veins. "As you can see I'm alive." He flinched as if I had slapped him hard enough to knock a few teeth loose, but I refused to feel sympathetic toward him. For me, his concern came eighteen years too late.

"I know you don't like me much, Lana. I don't blame you in the least for hating me, actually. When you were born, I wasn't a very nice person, more like a real bastard." He sighed. "I lost everything and I blamed you for it, even when I knew that you were the only innocent one in the whole damned mess."

"I never wanted your money," I spit the words at him.

"And I never planned on stopping the child support." He surprised me by admitting that. "It was just a ruse to force your mother to let me see you."

Despite myself, I found myself wanting to know more all of a sudden. "Why?"

Cole grimaced. "At the time I thought I was going to die of throat cancer. I wanted to make peace with everyone in my life, you included. That was before they removed the nodule on my vocals and discovered that it was benign."

"I'm so glad that when you found out you weren't going to kick the bucket you decided I wasn't worth your time after all." I rolled my eyes at him, angry with him and myself for even daring to wonder about that time in my life. "I think you should go now. I'm tired."

"I didn't mean to upset you, Lana. I'm sorry that I have." His face was full of remorse, but I wasn't willing to let myself care.

"Did you ever sort things out with your son?" I called after him before he had reached the door. The fact that I had a brother had never really mattered to me. Even at the age of eight, when I had first realized that I had a brother, I knew that the boy I shared blood with was a douche bag.

Cole turned. "No. His mother poisoned him against me. Now, even as successful as he is in the movie business, he isn't much to be proud of. Not like you, Lana. You, I have always been proud of. For not turning out like your mother, for growing up to be so mature and independent."

"Layla was a good role model. She raised me, took care of me, and did the things that you should have had the balls to do." The words came out full of venom. "You weren't man enough to take care of your responsibilities. Others had to do your job."

"I know." He wasn't making excuses and that made me even angrier, which was completely crazy.

"You don't deserve to be my father."

"I know that too."

"Stop it!" I shouted. "Just stop it!"

"Stop what, Lana?" he asked, his voice calm in my fury. "Stop agreeing with you? I know that I'm a piece of shit. I know that I let you down when I should have done everything in my power to protect you. Not a day goes by that I don't wake up hating myself because of what I did to you. Fuck, girl. I didn't even know your name until Jesse Thornton nearly tore my head off yesterday. And when I realized that the little girl I had tossed aside like yesterday's garbage was you... That my little girl had been so close to bleeding to death, and I hadn't gotten to tell you all the things I wanted—needed—to tell you, I lost it."

Angry, frustrating tears spilled down my cheeks, and I scrubbed them away with the hand that wasn't tangled in my IV line. "And you think that coming here and baring your soul will wipe away the past?" I shook my head. "It doesn't work like that, Cole."

"God, I know that, sweetheart. I know that nothing I say or do will ever make up for the past. I'm even prepared for you to hate me for the rest of your life... I just needed to talk to you. To tell you..." he blew out a long sigh that was full of regret. "I'm sorry for your loss, honey. And I hope that you and Stevenson are happy together. He doesn't deserve you, but if he makes you happy, then you hold on tight."

I opened my mouth to yell at him again, but nothing came out but a choked sob. Through my tears, I watched as my dad turned and walked out the door to my hospital room.

--

I spent three more days in the hospital. By that time, Nik had flown out with Mia and Lucy. I hadn't seen my baby sister since I had moved to New York, so it was a bitter sweet reunion when I got to see her. She was keeping her hair shorter now, all those long dark ringlets now short little curls that ended at her chin just added to her beauty.

My emotions were all over the place at the moment. The doctor told me that it was completely normal, that I would have some postpartum even though I hadn't been very far into the pregnancy. Seeing Mia, so beautiful and healthy, made my heart ache for the unknown little being that had been growing inside of me...

I was so glad to go home. I felt like I was going to go insane locked up in the hospital room. Instead of going back to my apartment, Drake asked me to go home to his. He wanted me to move in, and I was more than willing to do just that. I didn't want to spend a day away from him ever again if I could help it. Layla and Jesse tried to talk me into going back to California with them when they went home, but I couldn't. To me, New York was home now. I only hoped that Drake felt the same way.

Every night, Drake slept beside me. He held me close, and we talked like we had never talked before. I felt like I knew him inside and out now, but something was missing. He kissed me often, but never tried to take it further. Even when I got the green light from the doctor six weeks later, it was as if he was scared to touch me.

I didn't know what to think about that. I knew that he still wanted me, could feel his erection every time he kissed me. Each morning, I woke to his dick hard as a rock, twitching against my ass. When I tried to make things happen, he would always pull back. To say I was frustrated was the understatement of the century.

Other than being sexually frustrated, life was returning to normal. I was getting through my depression with Drake's help as well as help from my friends. Layla called every day to check in on me, and Lucy was constantly sending me crazy texts. Jesse was being a little overbearing, acting like the protective alpha male that he was.

"I just worry about you, Lana," he told me when I complained about it.

"I know, Jesse. And I love you for it," I told him as I gathered my books for the classes I had that day. "But you need to calm down a little before you have a stroke."

"Is he treating you good?" he demanded, still not over being pissed at his best friend. "I'll kill him if he isn't."

"He treats me like a princess," I assured my brother-in-law. "He loves me."

"That doesn't mean anything," Jesse muttered, and then I heard Layla saying something in the background. "Okay, okay. I'll talk to you tomorrow. Love you, Lana."

"Love you, Jesse."

Harper and I often had lunch together. I missed hanging out with her like we used to when I was living with her, but with her and Shane always together, I still saw quite a bit of her. Their relationship still had me stumped. I wasn't sure if they were sleeping together or not, if they were just friends or something more. Crazily enough, it was Harper that was giving Shane the runaround on their relationship and not the other way around. If anything I was sure that Shane was actually ready to settle down, if only Harper would open her eyes.

I saw Linc and Dallas regularly too. Linc was always up for a workout partner and Dallas was over at Drake's, often with Axton. The video for OtherWorld was coming up, and I was sure that Drake was going to throw a fit when he found out what Axton and his creative director for the video had planned. My tattoo was going to be a big part of it.

The day that Drake had seen my tattoo for the first time had been emotional for both of us. The first day I was home from the hospital he helped me shower. As I took off my shirt and he had seen my back he had lost it...

"Angel!" he exclaimed.

I glanced at him over my shoulder as I felt the temperature of the water. "Do you like it?" I had only really seen the end results the day before while I was still in the hospital. It was healing nicely, and I was really happy with the job the artist had done.

I had known what I wanted on my back for a while but hadn't decided on the design until I had found Drake's sketch pad. It was one he had drawn in while he was in rehab. All the pictures were of me, some had angel wings sticking from my back or wrapping around my body. Closer to the back there was a page of nothing but different wings, and I had torn it out and taken it with me.

My entire back was covered in a set of angel wings, each feather detailed and shadowed to look as if they were actually coming out from my back. Between the two wings, across my shoulders in curvy lettering were the words: *THE DEMON'S ANGEL*.

Trembling fingers traced over the words then lower over the defined detailing of each feathery angel wing. "It's beautiful," he whispered, lowering his head to kiss the ink.

I turned in his arms. "I love you, Drake. Never forget that."

"Ah, Angel. I love you." His lips brushed tenderly over my brow. "You make me complete."

Chapter 24
Drake

I was a mess.

I didn't know what the outcome of tonight would be, and I was terrified of the possible negative results. My entire future hung on the hinges of this one night, and I couldn't fail.

America's Rocker was doing better than the producers had ever hoped. Halfway through the season, Axton and I both had been asked to sign another contract for the next year. There was only one way I was doing it, and I was hoping to have my answer for the bigwigs before the end of the night.

Demon's Wings was preforming tonight as part of my contract for this season, and I was using it to my advantage. Emmie had helped me make the biggest of the arrangements, and I had spent days going over exactly how it was all going to pan out. Every last detail had been taken care of, and now all I had to do was wait.

Waiting fucking sucks!

Shane slapped me on the back as he came up behind me. We were back stage getting ready for the show, and the makeup artist was shooting me irritated glares because I kept sweating off the shit she put on me. "Bro! I can't believe you are doing this. I'm happy for you, man."

"Be happy for me later, after this night is over," I told him, waving the girl away when she tried to go for round three with some kind of brush to my face.

"I know how this night is going to end. So I'll be happy for you now and later." My brother grinned as he picked up a hair brush and smoothed out his hair. "I'm going out to sit with the girls. See you in a few."

I watched in the mirror as he walked toward the door that led out to the audience. When he reached it, he paused and turned around. "I really am happy for you, Dray. I love you, brother."

My throat felt tight and I had to clear it before I could speak. "I love you too."

I was on pins and needles over the next forty-five minutes. Never before had I been nervous to perform live, not to this extent. As the show went on and the last of the dwindling hopefuls took the stage, I thought I was actually going to throw up. When I should have been paying attention to the girl on stage singing her heart out for me and millions of viewers at home, my gaze kept drifting to the front row of the audience.

Layla and Lucy sat on either side of Lana, having flown out with Jesse to watch the show tonight. While Lucy had no clue what was about to happen, Layla did, and she shot me a wink when she saw me looking their way. Lana raised a brow when she saw that my attention was on her and not work, but she blew me a kiss.

Mia sat on Layla's lap and was entranced by the goings on around her. I was sure that one year old babies would normally be going crazy, wanting down to explore everything, but Mia was content to just sit on "Tee-tee Lay's" lap and watch while her mother took care of business backstage. Shane sat behind Lana with Harper, Dallas, and Linc. Lana's old roommates were still a big part of her life, and I was glad to have them here tonight for this. Harper waved and I nodded my head in her direction, wondering for the hundredth time if that girl was ever going to put my brother out of his misery. Shane had it bad. He didn't screw around these days, and it was all because of Harper...

Axton nudged my leg, and I turned around, realizing that the song was about to end and I was expected to give the first critique on the girl's performance. I don't know what exactly I said, I was working on only a half a brain, but it must have been good enough because everyone was cheering and clapping, agreeing with whatever it was I happened to say.

Ten minutes later, I was backstage, gearing up for the ending performance. My band brothers all pounded me on the back a few times, Jesse harder than the others because he still hadn't gotten completely over Lana's confession from months ago.

As Jesse stepped back, Emmie hugged me tight, wiping a tear away as she smiled up at me. "Good luck. I love you."

I dropped a kiss on top of her head. "Thanks, Emmie. For everything." Before I could say anything more, the host announced Demon's Wings and the audience went crazy. I rushed to take my place before the rotating stage turned.

Jesse was already starting us off before the stage was completely turned around. My knees felt weak as I let my fingers work across my Fender. The whole stage was in complete darkness and the fans in the audience were shouting because they knew the tune that we were playing, but it wasn't a Demon's Wings song.

My voice filled the speakers, coming out clear and steady. No one was expecting me to sing, and at first there was a pause in the crowd's reaction as they realized it was me and not Nik singing. *Heaven* was a clichéd song, one that a lot of guys proposed to their girlfriends with. But not many of them could sing it on stage in front of the entire world.

My eyes sought out Lana as soon as they adjusted to the lighting, but she was sitting too far back into the shadows, and I couldn't see her or anyone else. I had no clue what her reaction was, or if she even realized what I was doing as I continued to sing the song that Bryan Adams had made so popular.

Oh once in your life you find someone

Who will turn your world around
Bring you up when you're feelin' down
Now nothin' can change what you mean to me

My heart was literally beating me to death, and I could feel the sweat pouring from my face. If there was ever a time to want a drink it would have been now, but I had vowed that I was never going to touch another bottle in my life. I would not put myself in a position where I could possibly lose Lana again. The only whiskey I needed stared back at me in Lana's eyes every day.

I stepped forward letting Nik, who had been singing backup for me, take over. I reached into my jeans pocket and pulled out the box that I held the ring I had spent weeks searching for. I knew that my angel would never accept something over the top. The simple diamond I had chosen for her was perfect. Not ostentatious or even flashy.

It was a two carat, princess style cut diamond that suited Lana perfectly.

I moved toward the end of the stage and hopped down. The lighting was dim, but before long a spotlight was soon on me, and I could finally make out Lana's expression. Tears poured down her face, but she was smiling. That smile eased the tightness around my heart, and I fell to my knees in front of her.

My fingers were trembling as I opened the box. "I feel like I've waited my entire life to find you, and now that I have, I don't ever want to be without you. Will you marry me, Angel?"

With a sob she flung her arms around my neck. "Yes," she whispered through her tears. "Yes. Yes. YES!"

The crowd exploded into applause around us.

Lana

I had everything I could possibly want in life: a loving family, friends that meant the world to me, even a dad that I was trying to get to know now that I was learning to let go of the past and accept him as part of my future. It had been hard to do at first, but Cole really was trying hard to be a part of my life, and I was tired of fighting it.

It was impossible to be happier than I was right then.

I lay on our bed, my gaze on the hand that held the most incredibly beautiful engagement ring I had ever seen in my life. It looked so perfect on my finger, so right. With a contented sigh, I turned onto my stomach, impatiently waiting for my fiancé to come out of the bathroom where he had disappeared when we had gotten home just a little while ago.

The shower turned off and I pushed myself up against the pillows. A few minutes later, Drake came out of the bathroom with a towel wrapped tightly around his waist. My mouth went dry at the sight of him. I wanted to devour him that very second, thought for sure I would spontaneously combust if he didn't take me...

"Hey, beautiful." He placed a tender kiss on my forehead before turning toward the dresser to take out a pair of boxers.

I stared at his back for a full minute before I lost it. "Will you please make love to me?!?" I cried.

He turned around. "What?"

I bit my lip, hating that I was resorting to begging the man I loved to touch me. "Please, Drake. Make love to me." I got up on my knees and held out my hand to him.

Drake dropped the pair of boxers he had just pulled from his drawer and crossed over to me in two big steps. His fingers linked with mine, and I pulled him to me. "Why haven't you made love to me lately? Are you scared of hurting me?"

"A little." He kissed the tip of my nose, but his eyes were dark with suppressed desire. "But mostly it has been because I want to do things the right way this time. I want to make you my wife before we have sex again."

My heart melted and if it were possible I think I fell even more in love with the man. "That…" I swallowed the emotion clogging my throat and tried again. "That is really romantic, Drake."

His free hand wrapped around the ends of my hair and tilted my head back so I was looking up at him. "I love you, Angel. I ache to have you, don't ever doubt that. I just want to wait until we are married."

I grinned. "Okay then. Pack a bag. We are flying to Vegas."

His lips lifted as he returned my grin, but he was shaking his head. "We are going to have a real wedding. With a church, and a minister, and a giant cake that Lucy is going to get a stomachache trying to eat all of. You are going to have the most amazing wedding dress, and I will actually wear a tux. It's going to be amazing because that is what you deserve."

"Stop," I whispered, blinking in an attempt to keep the tears back. "Stop making me cry tonight."

One errant tear escaped, and he lowered his head to kiss it away. "I'll only ever make you cry for joy from now on. I swear it." His lips trailed down my cheek to my jaw, then lower finding that sensitive spot just behind my ear that made my knees weak. "And just because I want to wait for the sex doesn't mean we can't do other things," he murmured in a passion filled voice that sent delicious shivers up and down my spine.

A moan escaped me as he cupped my breast through the thin material of my camisole. My back arched, trying to get closer to his touch. "Please, Drake."

"Shh, Angel, I'll take care of you," he promised. "I will always take care of you."

He lifted me into his arms and laid me down against the pillows. I clung to his neck, forcing him to follow me. His towel disappeared and I let my hand drift down his hard stomach to the satin covered steel that lay between us. Drake bit back a curse as my fingers wrapped around him. "This is about you, Angel."

"No..." I shook my head "...this is about us." I tightened my hold on him and stroked upward. The head of his dick leaked his pre-cum, and I wiped it away with my thumb. "I'm going to take care of you too, Drake. Always."

Drake groaned as I stroked downward again, and his mouth found mine as he devoured my lips in a soul binding kiss. I kissed him back, relishing the taste of this man that held my heart in the palm of his talented hand. His hands didn't remain still as they stroked up and down my body, turning up the heat on a flame that was about to rage out of control.

My panties went flying as he ripped them off of me without breaking our kiss. Long, strong fingers were gentle as they parted the lips of my pussy, and his thumb skimmed over the ultra-sensitive ball of nerves. I cried out into his mouth and bit down on his bottom lip without realizing I was doing so.

He pulled back just a little, licking at his injured lip. "Easy, Angel." He grinned at me. "I'm not unbreakable."

"Sorry, babe," I touched trembling fingers to his swollen lip. "I want you so bad."

Blue-gray eyes darkened. "Me too. I've been dying to have you."

"I really love that you want to wait, Drake...but I think I'm going to go insane if you don't put your dick in me right now." I lifted my knees and spread my thighs wide, showing him how wet I was for him. "Show me how much you love me, Drake. Prove it to me right now."

"I don't have anything to protect you with, Angel."

I swallowed hard. "Do you want a baby Drake?" We hadn't really talked about the future and children. It wasn't a game changer for me because as long as I had Drake I didn't need anything else. But...

"I didn't think I did until you lost ours. The instant I knew that our child was growing inside of you and that we would never get to hold her..." He looked away, trying to hide his glazed eyes from me. "I want our child, Angel."

I rubbed my hands up and down his muscular arms. "Do you think it's too soon? Do you want to wait?"

He frowned, considering his answer hard before shrugging. "I think that we should just let fate decide for us." He brushed a tender kiss across my lips. "If it's meant to be, it will happen. Is that okay with you?"

My heart filled with even more love for him. "It's more than okay, Drake." I sat forward and kissed his chest right over his heart. "Make love to me, babe."

Epilogue

Lana

I was sound asleep when I felt him climb into bed with me. Sighing happily, I turned over and snuggled into my husband.

Strong arms pulled me even closer, and a scruffy jaw rubbed against my cheek as he brushed a kiss over my lips. Drake had been on a two week tour on the West Coast for the last two weeks, and I had missed him horribly. FaceTime and Skype just didn't cut it when I was so used to having the real thing holding me close every night.

"I missed you," he whispered gruffly.

"Missed you more," I told him, raising my hand to stroke my fingers through his shoulder-length hair. "I'm so glad you're home."

"Next time you are coming with me." I didn't get to go on tour with him often. School got in the way. Now that I was getting my Masters in Psychology it made touring harder on him because I didn't have a minute to spare so I could go with him.

"Only if next time isn't in the near future." I told him, fighting a yawn. I was exhausted. Sleep was my best friend these days. Normally, I would have been all over my husband after being without him for two whole weeks. And while I was already more than ready for him, I craved sleep even more.

"Emmie said something about a European tour in a few months," Drake murmured. "I'm not going unless you go with me."

My eyes snapped open and I pushed up to a sitting position before reaching over to turn on the lamp that sat on the table on my side of the bed. "You can't go."

Drake frowned up at me. My tone was forceful and I hadn't meant it to be, but then again, I hadn't been expecting to have this conversation at one o'clock in the morning. I had planned how I would talk to him about this, and now Emmie's tour plans were messing with it.

"Why not?" he asked, his brow cocked in that way that always made my mind blank.

"Because..." I sighed. "I have to tell you something."

"So tell me." He reached for my hands and entwined our fingers. The smile he gave me was full of all the love I knew he felt for me, the darkening of his blue-gray eyes attesting to how much he wanted me. "Then come here so I can make love to my wife."

I bit my lip, not scared of his reaction, but disappointed that I was telling him like this instead of how I had originally planned. "Fate decided it was time."

His brow furrowed for a moment as he tried to make sense of what I had just said. When it hit home, his whole face lit up. "Really? Oh my God! Angel, that's amazing." He pulled me down across his chest, being extra gentle as he kissed me. "I'm so happy," he whispered against my lips.

Tears spilled from my eyes as I hugged him close. "I just found out yesterday," I told him. "The doctor said that he thought everything looked great."

He pulled back, upset by my tears. "Why are you crying, Angel?"

"Because I didn't think it was going to happen, and now that it has, I'm so happy I can't contain my emotions." It felt like we had been trying for an eternity instead of just eighteen months. I knew that other couples had to try even longer to get pregnant, and I had even been prepared for it to never happen for us. But now I was overcome with so many emotions I was in overload. "I'm so happy, Drake."

"So am I, Angel." His eyes were glassy with his own suppressed emotions. "I thought the day that you married me was the happiest day of my life, but this...this is perfect."

"I want to tell Layla." It had been hard not to tell my sister my news earlier that day when she had called. I hadn't told anyone about the baby because I wanted Drake to be the first person who shared in my joy.

"Can you wait to call her in the morning?" He was rubbing my back in that way that always told me in was about to ravage me.

All thoughts of calling my sister faded, and I raised my head to meet his kiss. "I love you, Drake."

His tongue skimmed over my bottom lip. "I love you, Angel."

Drake

I woke alone in bed.

Frowning, I turned over and glanced at the clock on Lana's bedside table. It was after two. I had slept half the day away without meaning to. The flight home last night had really taken it out of me. Lana's news and the lovemaking that had followed drained me of what little energy I still had.

Groaning, I got out of bed and jumped into the shower. I needed to shave but decided to let it go until later, not wanting to spend another second away from my angel. Plans were already forming in my head. Take my expecting wife out for a nice late lunch, buy her a million things, maybe even do a little shopping for the nursery...

The thought of a nursery made me stop. Lana and I were still in the same apartment with Shane in one of the other bedrooms. Maybe it was time to find our own place? I would have to talk to Lana about it and maybe get Emmie to talk to some realtors for us.

After my shower, I tossed on boxers, old jeans, and a newer Demon's Wings T-shirt. I could smell something delicious coming from the kitchen, and my stomach grumbled, telling me I hadn't had a home cooked meal in two weeks. I opened the bedroom door...

Laughter was coming from the kitchen, and I frowned when I recognized it as Layla's. Jesse's deeper chuckle joined in followed by Lucy's giggles. I had just seen my band brother the day before as we had parted ways at LAX at the end of the tour. He hadn't said anything about coming out to New York.

I stopped just outside the door to the kitchen and looked in as the crowd milled around the island. Lucy was munching on cookies that were freshly baked. Jesse, never able to resist something freshly cooked by Lana, was stuffing his face with the chocolate chip goodness as well. Layla and Lana were leaning against the counter by the dishwasher. They hadn't seen each other since Christmas and it was now May.

"If I knew you guys were coming I would have gotten up," I told them as I stepped into the kitchen. "Hey, pretty girl." I dropped a kiss on top of Lucy's head then pulled Layla into my arms for a tight hug before kissing my angel. Finally, I turned to face my friend, band brother, and now my brother-in-law. It had taken Jesse a while to fully forgive me for what I had done to Lana—fuck, it had taken me a while to forgive myself—but things were finally back to normal with us. "Did you miss me that bad, bro?"

"So bad, man." He snorted.

"Actually, we had some news that we wanted to share." Layla said, and I turned to glance at her. She was smiling in a way that made me want to smile back. She looked over at her husband and the love shining in her eyes was only a mirror of what I always saw shining back at me when I looked into Lana's. "I thought that you guys would want to know that you are going to be having a couple nieces or nephews coming at the end of the year."

I blinked, not sure I had heard her correctly. Maybe my brain was still half asleep. "You're pregnant?"

"Yes." She grinned at my dazed look. "I'm pregnant and..."

"It's twins!" Jesse exclaimed, pride and love coating his words.

My gaze went to Lana who seemed to be more dazed than I was. Tears filled those whiskey eyes, and I rushed to pull her into my arms. "Okay?" I murmured.

Layla's excitement seemed to evaporate. "I'm sorry, Lana. I'm so insensitive. I should have realized that this would hurt you. You lost your baby..." She broke off, her chin trembling. "I just wanted to share our happy news with you."

"No." Lana shook her head at her sister. "I'm happy for you. So happy!" She scrubbed at her face. "And we have news of our own." She looked up at me and smiled through her tears. "We're having a baby too. Our due date is December fifteenth."

Layla gasped and then squealed. "Oh. My. God!" She pushed me away as she pulled Lana into her arms. "My due date is December sixteenth!"

"What?!?" Lana was laughing now, and the two sisters started jumping up and down in their excitement. "Layla, that's crazy!"

It was almost surreal, how happy I was as I watched my angel and seeing how happy she was in that moment. There was nothing in the world I would ever want more than to see her smiling. In that minute, I knew just how lucky I was. I had everything I would ever want, ever need right in front of me.

Jesse pounded me on the back. "Congratulations, man."

With a grin I turned to my friend. "You too, bro! I'm thrilled for you. Good work on the twins."

"So I'm going to be an auntie and a big sister. That is so cool," Lucy said, still munching on cookies.

My plans for the day were tossed out the window, but as I fell into bed that night with Lana, I didn't care. I was too happy, too content to worry about anything else but the perfect, warm ass snuggled into my aching crotch. "Thank you, Angel."

She was already half asleep. "Hmm?"

"Thanks for making me the happiest man in the world."

She sighed happily and pressed back against me. "You deserve it, babe."

Yeah, I thought as I closed my eyes. I was finally realizing that I really did deserve it.

Upcoming Books By Terri Anne Browning

The Rocker That Loves Me (Shane)
The Rocker That Holds Her (Nik)
The Rockers' Babies
The Rocker That Wants Me (Axton)

Made in the USA
Charleston, SC
22 February 2014